Brill and the Puffire Volcano

Brill and the Puffire Volcano

PEGGY DOWNING

Illustrated by
Anne Feiza

A WINNER BOOK

VICTOR BOOKS ®

A DIVISION OF SCRIPTURE PRESS PUBLICATIONS INC.
USA CANADA ENGLAND

The Exitorn Adventures
BRILL AND THE DRAGATORS
SEGRA AND STARGULL
SEGRA IN DIAMOND CASTLE
BRILL AND THE ZINDERS
SEGRA AND THE MAGICIAN
BRILL AND THE PUFFIRE VOLCANO

Cover illustration by Ed Sobieraj

Scripture quotations are from *The King James Version.*

Library of Congress Catalog Card Number: 89-60141
ISBN: 0-89693-734-8

VICTOR BOOKS
A division of SP Publications, Inc.
        Wheaton, Illinois 60187

CONTENTS

*For Kay Stewart
and Joan Biggar
with thanks*

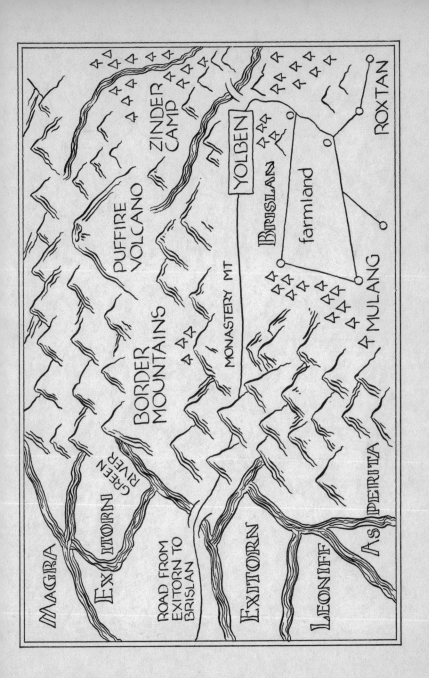

Trouble in Brislan 1

rill fitted an arrow into his bow at the archery range on Palatial Island.

"Hit the bull's-eye," called Segra.

"I'll try." He aimed at the target mounted on a bale of hay at the other end of the field. The released arrow whizzed through the air . . . and hit the outer circle.

He groaned. "I have to do better than that. I'm going to keep practicing until I can impress the archery master at our next lesson. Your turn, Segra."

But she didn't answer. She was staring intently at the moat ten feet below them. "Brill," she breathed, "I just saw a head!"

"What kind of a head?"

"A person's head."

"I don't see anything."

"He must be swimming underwater. Keep watching! He'll have to come up for air."

The glare of the sun on the water hurt Brill's eyes. "Why would anyone swim across the moat?"

"Because they don't want to cross the bridge. He must be a robber or a spy! Let's go closer so we can see him when he gets out of the water."

They walked to the edge of the island. A narrow stretch of beach was ten feet below them.

"There! I saw his head again." Segra pointed to the water.

"It might be an otter."

"No, it was a man."

"I didn't get a good look at it."

Segra ran along the bank closer to the spot where she saw the head.

Brill ran behind her saying, "Segra, why don't you run back and get some soldiers? This fellow might be dangerous."

"All the more reason for us both to confront him. We're armed. We can capture him." Segra stopped and stepped behind a bush. "Don't let him see us yet. As soon as he steps out of the water, we'll aim our arrows at him and demand his surrender."

Brill watched the water. This time he saw a blond head bob up from the water. The man looked around, then stood in the shallow water by the beach and waded ashore.

Segra stepped to the edge and called down to him, "Surrender, or we'll shoot."

The wet man looked up at them. "Don't shoot. I don't mean anyone any harm. I need to see your king on a very important matter."

Brill whispered, "Be careful. It may be a trick."

Segra called, "Come up the bank slowly. My friend is aiming an arrow at you, so don't try to escape."

Brill swallowed. He put an arrow in his bow and stood ready to shoot, even though the thought of killing or hurting another person made him feel sick inside.

The man climbing the steep bank kept slipping back, but finally he grabbed hold of a shrub on the edge and pulled himself to the level where Segra and Brill stood. He was on his knees, and his wet clothes were covered with dirt from his climb.

"Don't make any sudden moves," barked Brill, trying to look fierce rather than scared.

"Why'd you swim across the moat?" demanded Segra.

The man took a deep breath. "I was being followed, and swimming seemed the only way to keep away from my pursuers." He sat on his heels and looked at them with a frown clouding his deep-blue eyes.

"Where are you from?" asked Brill.

"Brislan, across the mountains."

Segra stepped closer to him. "What's your name?"

"Trant, former prince of Brislan."

Segra cried, "I'm your cousin—Segra! I've always wanted to meet you."

"I've heard about you, Segra. It's your father I must see."

Brill scowled. "We'd better make sure he's who he says he is."

Segra whispered, "Look at the pearl buttons on his

velvet tunic, and the lace band on his hose.* He's wearing an emerald ring. He may be muddy, but he's dressed like a prince."

Trant took off his outer tunic. "Perhaps the June sun will dry the mud so I can brush it off before I meet the king."

"Tell me why you're here," begged Segra as she sat on the grass beside him.

Brill stood clutching his bow, ready to defend Segra if this handsome young man turned out to be a criminal after all.

Trant began, "I had to flee from Brislan. Uncle Vashton had my father, Choner, killed and then proclaimed himself king. I was out hunting when a friend reported the news to me." He looked across the water. "I barely escaped with my life."

"That's terrible!" cried Segra. "What about your mother and sister?"

"Uncle Vashton is holding them prisoners." Prince Trant's voice shook as if he were fighting tears. When he regained his composure, he said, "Vashton planned to kill me. He knows many people want me to succeed my father as king. That's why I had to run away. Oh, I wish I could have taken my mother and sister with me, but I couldn't go back to the palace without being captured and executed. I don't think Uncle Vashton will kill them as long as he sees a chance for a ransom."

"Do you know who was following you?" asked Segra.

He shook his head. "I was almost to your capital when horsemen galloped up behind me wearing Brislan uniforms. Luckily my stallion could outrun them, and I managed to lose them in the city streets. I didn't dare go to the bridge for fear they'd be watching for me there."

"Where is your horse?" asked Brill.

"In a stable at Maple Inn."

"I'll get a stable boy to fetch him," offered Brill.

"Let's sneak in the palace the back way." Segra stood. "Come with us, Trant. Brill will get you some clean clothes."

Trant jumped up. "With a bath and dry clothes, I'll feel better. Oh, I hope your father will know how to help my mother and sister."

As they walked back to the castle, Brill remarked, "I didn't know you had relatives in Brislan, Segra."

She explained, "Long before I was born, Aunt Herla married Prince Choner of Brislan. She was only fourteen, and Father has told me that Grandfather didn't want his daughter to marry Choner and move so far away. Brislan is across the mountains, and the journey is not an easy one."

"Why did he give his permission?" asked Brill.

"Aunt Herla fell in love with Choner when he visited here, and she was determined to marry him. It's such a romantic story.... We don't hear from Aunt Herla very often. I've always wished I could meet her and my cousins."

"I've wanted to meet you, too," said Trant.

"Tell me about your sister, Julnie," said Segra. "What's she like?"

"Julnie is fourteen, a little shorter than you." Trant's face clouded. "It must be very hard for her to be locked up."

"I can't wait to meet her. O Trant, I feel so sorry about your father. I wish I had known him. He must have been a wonderful man."

"He was. He'd never hurt anyone, and when I think how his brother plotted against him, it makes my blood boil."

Segra looked at Brill. "We have to rescue Aunt Herla and Julnie."

Brill swallowed. "But how?"

"We'll figure out a way," said Segra.

Trant sighed. "Vashton has soldiers everywhere in Brislan. He knows he has lots of enemies."

They came to the castle, and Brill took Trant to his room, where he ordered a bath prepared. He gave Trant his best green tunic. Trant was five feet ten—about two inches taller than Brill—but other than being a little short, Brill's clothes fit him.

Segra knocked and told them the king was waiting in his private sitting room.

"He's already received a letter asking for a ransom," she said when they came out. "It was probably the king's messengers who were chasing you, Trant. We have to keep you away from any place where Vashton's men might see you."

Trant stepped closer to Segra. "So the king already knows what's happened?"

"Yes, but he wants to hear your side of the story."

In the sitting room, Trant told his story to the king and queen.

The king's forehead creased in a worried frown. "As long as Vashton is ruling your country, you must stay here," he said.

"Thank you, Uncle Silgar. But I plan to go back to fight Vashton as soon as Mother and Julnie have been released. Any show of force now could lead Vashton to kill them."

"What ransom is Vashton demanding?" asked Segra.

"The letter is from my sister Herla." The king read aloud:

> Dear Silgar,
>
> My daughter and I are being held prisoners in the castle at Brislan by King Vashton, who now rules. My husband, Choner, is dead. King Vashton will release us for a ransom of one pound of gold and a dozen large jewels. My son, Trant, has disappeared, and they say he is dead.
>
> Please help us.
>
> Love from your sister,
> Herla

"Your mother thinks you're dead" cried Queen Nalane.

"Perhaps my friends started that rumor, hoping it would keep Vashton from chasing me. But I'm sorry Mother has to endure more sorrow."

"She doesn't mention how King Choner died," observed Brill.

"She wouldn't dare accuse Vashton in the letter," said Trant. "I'm sure he read it before it was sent."

Segra spoke. "Father, Brill and I want to take the ransom to King Vashton. We'll dress like peasants so no one will suspect we're carrying a ransom."

King Silgar looked at his daughter sternly. "Segra, we have talked about this before. You are heir to the throne. Your business is here learning to be a queen—not traipsing across the mountains endangering your life."

"But I get bored at the castle. I like excitement."

"I don't know whom I shall send to Brislan, but it won't be you. This could be a dangerous mission. We can't trust Vashton. I'm not even sure he'll release Herla and Julnie if we do send a ransom." He looked at Trant.

"I'm not sure either, but I don't know any other way of getting my mother and sister out alive."

King Silgar stroked his beard. "Herla and Julnie are worth more to me than any amount of gold. If only I knew what Vashton will do."

"O Father, please let me go," cried Segra. "I want to help my cousin Julnie and Aunt Herla."

King Silgar repeated his decision. "Segra, if I died without an heir, the country would not have a leader. Please understand what chaos that could bring." He turned to Trant. "I'm afraid the messengers from Brislan will report to King Vashton where you are, and that may make negotiations more difficult."

Trant shook his head. "They weren't close enough to be sure of my identity. Even if they think they saw me, they probably won't tell Uncle Vashton, because he will be furious at them for not catching me. He's known for his bad temper."

Queen Nalane said, "Silgar, Trant looks very tired. Can't some of this talk wait until tomorrow?"

"Yes, you're right." King Silgar rang for a servant to show Trant to a room and bring him food.

The king looked at the others. "Whoever takes the ransom to King Vashton must be someone I can trust."

Brill felt prickles run up his back. *I'm the logical one to go. I already know how important it is to keep the mission a secret. I am a duke. Dukes serve their countries with heroic deeds—even if they are scared.*

His voice cracked as he spoke. "I'll go, Your Majesty. Perhaps Grossder will come with me. We'll bring back your sister and niece."

King Silgar looked at Brill then stood and put his hand on his shoulder. "Do you realize the danger?" he asked quietly. "It will be a long, hard journey, and King Vashton is not to be trusted."

"I know."

Segra squeezed his hand. "O Brill, you're so brave. God will guide you."

But fear clutched at Brill's stomach like an icy hand.

The Journey Begins 2

rill slipped away to think over the rash promise he had just made. As he walked down the hall, he felt Zack, a Zinder, tug on his tunic.

"Take me along to Brislan," he begged in his high-pitched voice.

"Zack! You shouldn't be sneaking around listening to other people's conversations!" scolded Brill.

Zack grinned. "Sometimes I'm glad to be so small that no one notices me."

Brill squatted down to be closer to eye level with the boy, a foot-and-a-half high. Zack had lived in the castle over a year, ever since he had been rescued from the evil magician Umber, who had kept him a prisoner and forced him to help him in his magic shows.

"I want to go across the mountains," repeated Zack.

"The king sent soldiers with you last summer to the forests beyond the mountains," reminded Brill, "but you couldn't find any other Zinders."

"I would have found them if I hadn't fallen from that tree and broken my leg."

"They had to carry you all the way back—remember?"

"But my leg is fine now, and the weather's getting warmer. Next time I won't climb tall trees—not until I've practiced climbing again."

"Why haven't you taken our advice and let Stargull* take you back? He could get you there in a hurry." The large white bird flew among the mountains and islands, stopping to visit Brill and Segra frequently.

Zack stamped his foot. "I'm not letting a bird clutch me in his talons and carry me through the air. I don't care if he has lifted Zinders before."

"I'm going on an important mission," explained Brill. "I won't have time to find your people."

"If you let me ride across the mountains to the forest, I'll find the Zinders myself."

"But what if you can't find them? You won't be able to survive alone in the forest."

Zack stood as tall as his small frame would allow. "Of course I can. I know the edible plants and how to keep warm in the coldest weather. Please, ask the king if I can go along."

The pleading look in Zack's eyes stayed with Brill even after he went to bed that night. As he tossed and turned, he thought of all the dangers he would be facing. What if Vashton planned to take the ransom and kill the messenger? If he had killed his own brother, he wouldn't mind killing a duke from Exitorn.

* * * * *

The next morning Brill found King Silgar in the throne room, studying a map of the border mountains and Brislan.

"Trant drew this map." With his finger Silgar traced the road from the Exitornian capital to Yolben, the capital of Brislan. "It won't be hard to find." He handed Brill the map.

"Thank you." He paused. "Sire, Zack wants to go too. He thinks he can find his people if he gets back to the forest where they live."

"That's an excellent idea. You can tell people you're taking Zack back to his people." The king leaned forward. "When can you be ready to leave?"

"I'll talk to Grossder this morning. I hope to leave first thing tomorrow."

"Fine. I'll order a stable boy to prepare supplies." The king put his hand on Brill's shoulder. "I'd advise you to make sure Herla and Julnie are safe before you give King Vashton the ransom."

Brill nodded. "Yes, Your Majesty."

After breakfast Brill walked to the cathedral* in the city where his friend Grossder worked and attended classes. Brill found him hoeing in the back garden.

Grossder looked up and a wide smile broke out on his round face. "Brill, it's good to see you."

"I came to see if you can take time off for an adventure."

Grossder gave a crooked smile. "If it's a dangerous one, I'd rather stay here and work in the garden."

"I don't think it'll be very dangerous." He dropped his voice. "I have to cross the Border Mountains to Brislan to pay a ransom and get the king to release two captives. But you don't need to face the king. I'll do that."

Grossder looked thoughtful. "It's strange, but our bishop said he needed someone to deliver a message to the monastery* near Brislan. Nobody volunteered, but he said God would find someone. Do you think I'm that person?"

Brill nodded. "It sounds like it."

"Will anybody else be going?"

"Just Zack, the Zinder. He wants to look for his people."

Grossder thought a moment. "When do we leave?"

"Tomorrow. As soon as you get your saddlebags packed, meet me at the castle. We'll find a horse for you."

Brill returned to his room to load his saddlebags. He wished Segra were going too. Her bravery gave him courage.

After dinner that evening, King Silgar gave Brill the ransom—a pound of gold pieces plus a dozen gems including diamonds, emeralds, and rubies. They were sewn between two layers of leather in a belt.

The king said, "This is a generous ransom. These jewels and the gold are worth a great deal."

"What if he wants more?" asked Brill.

"This is what Vashton asked for. He'll be satisfied unless he's completely unreasonable."

Brill rubbed sweaty palms together and turned to

Segra. "Good—good-bye, Segra."

She caught his hand. "Please, take care of yourself and hurry back." Her eyes glistened with tears.

"I will," he promised, holding both her hands for a long moment. They walked into a hallway.

"I'd like to sneak away with you," whispered Segra, "but I have to obey my father." She sighed. "He's right when he says my most important duty is to my country. I'll keep praying for you."

"Thanks, Segra. Good-bye." Brill headed in the opposite direction for his room. Two women servants were talking to the side up ahead.

"It's June already, and we should soon be hearing plans for a wedding now that Princess Segra is fifteen."

Brill slowed his steps as he passed the women.

The other one added, "I've heard that the groom will be Prince Oplack, for he's the only eligible prince from a friendly country."

Brill clenched his fists. *I knew this would happen! I may love Segra, but I can't marry a princess. I was born in a peasant's family even though I'm now a duke.*

Tears welled up in his eyes as he entered his room. *I can't go away now—not if what those servants say is true! What if I come back and find Segra betrothed* to Prince Oplack?* But Brill knew he could not break his promise. He had to forget his own dreams and concentrate on rescuing Segra's aunt and cousin. He crawled into his bed and stared at the black ceiling with sleepless eyes.

* * * * *

He, Zack, and Grossder left with the first light of

morning. Segra was nowhere around. The young men dressed as peasants, but Brill carried better clothes in his pack to wear when he met the king. He sat behind Zack on Comet and pulled the lead line of the pack pony. Grossder's mare trotted beside Comet as they rode out to the country.

Brill looked back at the castle and tried to swallow the lump in his throat. He wished his mission were over and he were returning to Segra. He thought of her tears when they had said good-bye last night. Did they mean she really loved him, or was she merely unhappy about missing an adventure?

Zack interrupted his thoughts. "I don't like horses. They're too wide and too high off the ground—not the right size for a Zinder."

"Comet will take us across the mountains a lot faster than you can walk," reminded Brill.

"I know. I'm glad we're finally going. I've been longing to go back to the forest for such a long time. Why do big people live in boxes when there's a whole beautiful world out there?"

"That world drops rain and snow and blows bitter cold air," reminded Grossder.

Zack laughed. "You big people are soft, but Zinders are tough. Rain or snow won't hurt us. When I was little, we lived in a big maple tree. Mother tied me to a wide branch and sang me to sleep." Zack began to hum a high, slow melody.

They spent the first night in the inn at Korfet. The next morning they followed a narrow road that led gradually upward toward the Border Mountains. By the time they reached higher elevations, a chill, strong wind blew off the snow from the surrounding peaks.

Grossder shouted above the howl, "When I deliver the message to the monastery in a few days, I'll ask for shelter for the night."

"How will we find the monastery, anyway?" questioned Brill.

"The bishop said we'll see it from the road. It's on top of a flat mountain west of Brislan."

"A hot meal and shelter would feel good."

Four weary days later they spotted the stone building on top of a mesa* in the distance.

"Let's stay for a while," suggested Grossder. "I'm saddle sore."

"We can't stay more than one night," said Brill. "Don't forget the prisoners."

Grossder looked at the sky. "Let's hurry before it starts to pour. Look at that black cloud spreading over us."

"Rain won't hurt me." Zack laughed. "Does rain melt big people?"

"It's uncomfortable to be all wet," pointed out Grossder. "I prefer to take baths in a tub with warm water and soap, but I suppose dirty Zinders have to depend on rain to wash them once in awhile."

"We bathe in streams," shouted Zack.

Brill scowled. "This isn't rain. It's gray dust! It's sticking to my clothes." He tried to brush it off.

"We can't see the monastery anymore," cried Grossder.

Brill sneezed as some of the powder got in his nose. Zack looked puzzled. "I've never heard of anything like this before."

At last they came to the rock mountain where the monastery stood. The air was clearer now. Zack spoke excitedly. "I remember seeing that building when I was little. We must be close to where I used to live. I'm going to start looking for my people right now. Stop Comet so I can get off."

"Don't get lost," warned Brill.

"Lost in the forest? Don't be silly! I can find all the food and shelter I need."

Brill reined in the horse and dismounted. He lifted Zack down and watched him scamper away.

"Good luck," called Brill.

Zack waved and disappeared into the trees.

"I hope he doesn't run into any wolves or bears," said Grossder.

They tethered their horses in a grassy meadow at the base of Monastery Mountain. The tether was long enough so the horses could drink from a nearby stream. Brill and Grossder walked up a steep trail, then up stairs cut in a sheer cliff.

Finally they reached the top. Grossder was gasping. "I don't like climbs like that. One misstep and you're smashed on the rocks below. Let's go."

Grossder led the way to the double door in the low stone building and knocked.

A monk* wearing a brown robe and hood opened the door and motioned for them to step inside. "Are you seeking shelter?" he asked.

"I bring a message from the bishop of Exitorn." Grossder handed him his letter.

The monk read the name and smiled. "Welcome to our humble home. Our abbot* is a good friend of Bishop Oliber. Wait here. I'll tell the abbot of your arrival."

The monk returned with a man he introduced as Father Mekdell.

"Welcome, boys. I will have a room prepared for you. How long can you stay?"

"Just tonight," answered Grossder. "We're on our way to Brislan."

Brill said, "Sir, as we were riding up here, a strange gray powder was falling through the air. Do you know what it was?"

The monk nodded gravely. "I surely do. Come with me, and I'll show you where it comes from." He led them through a long corridor and out the back way, where monks were working in a garden.

"Do plants grow well up here?" asked Grossder.

"Yes, indeed. The volcanic ash* from Puffire Volcano is good for plants."

"There's a volcano here?" Brill's eyes widened.

"That's where the gray powder comes from. Puffire has been acting up lately." He shook his head. "It looks serious. A short time ago gray clouds of ash bubbled up from its top as if it's getting ready for something bigger."

They walked past pens where monks were feeding chickens and pigs.

Father Mekdell whispered to the boys, "I can't introduce you because these monks have taken vows of silence."

At the edge of the mesa, they had a sweeping view of the surrounding mountains. The highest peaks wore mantles of snow. The valleys were dark green with thick forests.

Suddenly Father Mekdell pointed to the largest snow-covered peak. "Look, Puffire is smoking again!"

Brill watched a plume of gray smoke rise from the volcano's top. It widened and rose higher and higher.

"I never saw anything like that," said Grossder in an awed tone.

Brill stared at the gray cloud which was now beginning to dissipate in the light wind. Excitement and fear stirred inside him.

Father Mekdell quietly said, "You must be careful. You'll be passing closer to Puffire as you go to Brislan."

Brill Meets King Vashton **3**

rossder looked at Father Mekdell. "Perhaps we'd better turn back."

"I can't do that," exclaimed Brill. "I must help Queen Herla and Julnie."

"Volcanoes are unpredictable. No one knows what they'll do," said Father Mekdell.

"Does the smoke mean it might start spilling out hot lava*?" asked Grossder.

"I've been reading our old records," answered Father Mekdell. "Hot lava doesn't usually overflow Puffire's crater.* However, a few hundred years ago it exploded, killing many people with hot gases and ash.

28

Earthquakes shook the ground, and floods and mud-flows ran down the mountain when the heat melted the snow."

Grossder looked terrified. "You think it might do that again?"

Father Mekdell shrugged. "We don't know."

"Is hot ash as bad as burning lava?" asked Brill.

"Explosive eruptions are more dangerous. Flowing lava causes fires and destruction, but most of the time people can get out of the way, because lava usually moves slowly."

Brill stared at the dirty snow on Puffire.

Grossder muttered, "I'd sure like to go home."

Father Mekdell put his hand on his shoulder. "Let's pray the volcano will go back to sleep without doing any damage."

He led them back to the main building where the monks were gathering at a large table for their evening meal. The silence was eerie. Brill wondered if the monks who had taken a vow of silence were right. Does God try to tell us things, but we talk too much to hear Him?

Father Mekdell asked a blessing on the food, and then began passing hot vegetable soup and black bread around the table.

Brill enjoyed the food, but he was still a bit hungry when his portion was gone.

After dinner a thin young man led them to the chapel for vespers.* The abbot read from the Bible and preached a short sermon.

Afterward they thanked Father Mekdell for his hospitality and told him they planned to leave at dawn.

* * * * *

They arose the next morning when the four o'clock prayer bell rang. The June sky had begun to lighten just enough for them to see as they descended the mountain and returned to their horses. They ate a quick meal from their packs.

They looked toward Puffire as they rode, but it was hidden by thick clouds. That night they camped in a grove of trees outside the capital city of Yolben.

"I'm going to see the king in the morning," said Brill. "Will you keep the ransom for me?"

"I don't want to stay here alone," objected Grossder.

Brill took out Trant's map. "There's a cathedral in Yolben. Why don't you go there?"

"Good idea," Grossder agreed. "I'd like to see it."

"I don't trust Vashton, so I don't want the ransom with me until I've talked with him," explained Brill. "If he's ruthless enough to murder his brother, he might take the ransom by force."

"I'll keep the ransom until you need it," promised Grossder.

Brill spread his bedroll on the ground and lay down. "I wonder if Zack found any other Zinders."

"I wish he had stayed with us. He could keep me company while you're talking to Vashton." Grossder pulled his blankets tight around his neck.

Brill nodded. "I miss him. I hope he's safe."

The two soon dropped off to sleep. Brill had a terrible dream that Vashton was violently shaking him and screaming, "I'll make you give me the ransom!"

He awoke to find that the shaking was real. He jumped up in the darkness. "Earthquake!" he called.

Flashes of orange lightning danced at the summit

of Puffire Volcano, brightening a bubbling cloud of ash. The earth trembled again. Brill could hear the horses neighing and pawing at the ground. He ran over to Comet and patted her. "You'll be all right."

"What'll we do?" yelled Grossder.

Brill shivered. "Pray."

They prayed, then watched until the mountain disappeared in darkness and the earth stopped shaking. They returned to wrap themselves in their blankets, which were covered with a thin coating of ash.

The next morning Brill awoke with the queasy stomach he got when facing impending doom.

Grossder pulled out bread and cheese from the pony's pack. "Maybe King Vashton will invite us to a palace banquet tonight," he said hopefully.

"Not likely."

"Want some?" Grossder held out some bread and cheese.

"I'm not hungry."

"You scared?" asked Grossder.

"I'm more afraid of Vashton than I am of Puffire," he admitted.

"Do you think Vashton will kill you? Is that why you're scared?"

Brill shrugged. "I don't know what to expect." He went to the river, bathed as best he could, and put on his clean, blue tunic.

"Now you look more like a duke," said Grossder.

At that moment the ground gave another tremor. A gray cloud arose above the volcano's crater. Brill spoke crossly to Puffire. "I don't need you shaking and smoking. I have enough to worry about."

Grossder laughed. "I hope it heard you and goes

back to sleep until we get away from here."

After they repacked their gear, they mounted their horses and rode into the walled city. The gates stood open. Soldiers looked down at them from the top of the walls, but people were allowed to pass in and out freely.

Brill looked at the map Trant had drawn for him. "The cathedral's this way," he said.

Grossder pointed. "There's the spire.*"

They threaded their way through narrow streets until they reached the cathedral. Brill paid a groom to take care of their horses in a large stable at the back of the grounds.

They entered the cathedral and prayed. Then Brill arose from his knees and whispered, "I'll meet you here when my business with the king is finished."

Grossder nodded. "I'll keep praying for you."

"Thanks." Brill walked toward the castle which stood in the middle of town. Thick walls surrounded the royal headquarters.

One of the soldiers guarding the gate demanded, "What's your business?"

"I have a message for the king."

"You alone?" asked the soldier.

"Yes, I'm alone." *Very alone. Well, except God.*

The soldier signaled to two other men who raised the metal portcullis.* Brill walked under the spiked gate. He crossed the courtyard and was again challenged at the castle entrance.

"I have a message from the King of Exitorn," he explained.

A page* led him to the great hall and motioned toward a bench by the door. "Wait there until you're called."

Two golden thrones with red cushions stood on a raised dais* at the far end of the rectangular room. King Vashton sat on one throne. His red velvet tunic stretched tautly across his plump figure. Above his long, sharp-nosed face, a jeweled crown perched on his sand-colored hair.

The king was talking to three men in an agitated way. "I want you to find every rebel and put them in prison," he shouted.

"It's hard to tell," said a tall man.

"We fear that some who act loyal are not," added another man.

The king punctuated each sentence with forceful gestures. "We must have spies who will report to us every time they see something suspicious."

The men stepped closer to the king and conferred in low tones as though discussing secret plans.

Brill watched King Vashton, noting his angry gestures. He wondered if he should slip away and return when the king was in a better mood. But he had to get the prisoners released as soon as possible.

Finally the three men left, and a page led Brill to the throne.

"Duke Brill from Exitorn," the page announced.

Brill bowed. "King Silgar sends greetings, Your Majesty."

Vashton stared for a while at Brill with pale blue, hypnotic eyes. "Peaceful greetings, I presume."

"Oh, yes, Your Majesty."

"But your king has sent you for some purpose other than greeting me, I presume."

"King Silgar has received a message from his sister Herla." Brill's throat felt tight. "She wrote that she and

her daughter are being held for ransom."

A trace of a smile crossed Vashton's thin lips. "Are you offering me a ransom, Duke Brill?"

"Yes, Your Majesty—in exchange for Herla and Julnie."

"What did you bring? How much does Silgar value his sister?"

"First, I would like to see Queen Herla, please."

Vashton roared. "I give the orders around here. Show me the ransom!"

Brill tried to keep his voice steady. He couldn't let Vashton see his terror. "I don't have it with me."

"Where is it?" he demanded. "Did you bring soldiers to guard it?"

"No, I've come in peace. But I have orders to see Queen Herla and Julnie. If they are all right, I'll pay the ransom you asked for and take them back to Exitorn."

"But first I must see the gold and jewels."

"Will you promise to release the captives when I give you the ransom?" persisted Brill.

"I promise nothing!" Vashton roared. "You have two choices. Either return to Exitorn empty-handed or bring me the ransom."

He nodded toward a soldier, who took Brill's arm in his strong grip and hurried him out of the castle.

Brill glanced behind him to see if the soldier were following him, but he was standing by the gate talking to two other soldiers.

Hurrying toward the cathedral, Brill kept looking back. Those two soldiers were heading in his direction.

Brill ducked down a narrow street and ran. Why was he being followed? Perhaps King Vashton didn't believe him when he said he had no soldiers with him.

Out of breath, Brill ducked between two wooden houses. He had zigzagged through so many streets he had no idea where he was. He peeked out, but he couldn't see any soldiers.

A small boy looked at him curiously. "Are the soldiers after you?" he asked.

Brill nodded. "But I haven't done anything wrong."

"King Vashton's soldiers chase good people, too."

The boy's mother came to the doorway of their small house and pulled her son inside.

"Where's the cathedral?" called Brill.

She didn't answer him. She only scolded her son: "Don't let me ever see you talking to strangers."

Then Brill looked up and saw the cathedral spire, and felt foolish for asking the question. He rushed through the narrow streets, keeping on the alert for soldiers. Whenever he saw one, he went the other way. None of them chased him, so apparently these soldiers were not hunting for him. He found Grossder inside the cathedral.

"Come with me," whispered Brill.

Grossder stood, then sat down.

"What's wrong?" Brill frowned.

"I felt dizzy. I'll be all right in a minute."

Brill sat beside him and whispered his story.

"What are you going to do?" Grossder asked.

"I have to return to the castle with the ransom."

"I don't think you should trust Vashton. He might take the ransom and throw you in prison or kill you."

"That's what scares me."

Grossder untied the belt holding the ransom. "Why don't you go back to King Silgar and tell him the only language Vashton understands is force."

"I can't do that."

Grossder froze. "A soldier just came in, and he's watching us."

Brill hit his forehead with his palm and hissed, "I thought I had given them the slip." He glanced back. "He's looking the other way. Quick, let's get out of here."

They slipped out a side door and walked behind the stable. Grossder gave Brill the heavy belt.

"Thanks." Brill noticed how pale Grossder was. "Are you all right?"

Before Grossder could answer, four soldiers closed in on them. "The king wants to see you," declared one.

"I'm on my way to the castle," said Brill. "You don't want my friend."

"We have orders to bring you and your companions to the king."

One of the soldiers unsheathed his sword. "March," he ordered.

Hostages

Soldiers gripped the boys' upper arms and hurried them toward the castle. Curious townsfolk stared. "Must be robbers," one said loudly.

"The one in fine clothes doesn't look like a robber," screeched a woman.

"He could have stolen the clothes."

Brill's face felt hot with shame. He wanted to shout, *I'm no robber,* but the jeering people would only laugh.

He hadn't meant to involve Grossder in danger. He prayed, *Please, Lord, make Vashton release the captives when I give him the ransom. Don't let any harm come to Grossder.*

The soldiers jerked the boys to a stop before Vashton's throne. "Is this the only person traveling with you?" demanded the king.

"Yes, Your Majesty," answered Brill. "He came along to keep me company. Please, let him go."

Vashton stared at Grossder. "Speak the truth, boy. Are there others with you?"

Grossder cleared his throat. "No, Your Majesty. We're the only ones who came to Yolben."

Vashton turned his attention to Brill. "Show me the ransom."

Brill untied his belt and pushed the gold pieces and gems from the inside onto a small table by the throne.

The king examined the diamonds, rubies, emeralds, and gold pieces. He glared at Brill. "Is this all?" he demanded.

"Yes, Your Majesty." Brill spoke clearly, trying to hide his fear. "It's what you asked for."

"I asked for *large* jewels," he roared. "A queen and a princess are worth more than this." He held one of the diamonds up to the light. "Not even perfect."

"King Silgar is not rich. He sent as much as he had."

"Nonsense! He can tax his people more. I must have perfect jewels which are twice as large before I will release Herla and Julnie."

Brill protested, "These jewels and gold are worth a great deal."

"I know what they're worth, and it's not enough." Vashton nodded toward Grossder. "You can carry that message to Silgar."

"We will," agreed Grossder.

Brill added, "We'll return with Silgar's answer as soon as possible."

"*We?* I have other plans for you, Duke Brill. You'll join Herla and the princess as a hostage until your king pays a suitable ransom."

Brill gulped, fighting waves of panic. Vashton smiled as if he enjoyed seeing the fear in Brill's eyes.

Grossder, more pale than ever, stepped close to Brill. "I can't find my way alone."

"Nonsense. Just follow the road. Begone, young man, before I decide to lock you up and send soldiers on my mission."

Grossder bowed and scuttled away.

Vashton called a soldier. "Take Duke Brill to the hostages. He'll stay there until I receive a suitable ransom from his country."

The soldier led Brill down a long corridor on the ground floor. Brill wondered if there would ever be enough ransom, or if greedy Vashton would keep demanding more and more.

At the end of the hall, two soldiers guarded a carved door.

"Somebody to see the ex-queen." The soldier pushed Brill toward the door.

"She doesn't get visitors," said one guard.

"This isn't a visitor. He's a fellow hostage. Open the door. King's orders."

The guard unlocked the door, and Brill stepped into a comfortable, well-furnished suite* of rooms. The door slammed behind him.

Julnie, a pretty girl with shoulder-length, reddish-brown hair, stared up at him from a chair. "Who are you?"

"Duke Brill from Exitorn. I brought your ransom, but King—"

Julnie ran to a door and opened it. "Mother! Come quick. A man from Exitorn is here."

Queen Herla, wearing a green velvet dress, hurried from her bedroom to the sitting room. "Do you come from my brother Silgar?" she asked.

Brill bowed before the slender queen. "Yes, I do, Your Majesty. King Silgar sent me here with a ransom, but King Vashton is demanding larger jewels."

"I knew Vashton would be unreasonable." Queen Herla sat on a carved chair. "He killed my husband and possibly my son—out of greed." She dabbed at tear-filled eyes with a lace handkerchief.

Brill whispered, "Trant is safe in Exitorn."

"You've seen him?" Herla exclaimed.

"Yes. He's fine."

"Praise God! I've been so worried." She smiled at Brill, then whispered, "I hope you didn't tell Vashton where Trant is."

"Of course not."

Julnie pouted. "I'm glad Trant escaped, but I wish we could leave too. We've been locked up ever since Father was killed." Her voice caught in a sob.

"King Vashton has sent my companion back to Exitorn for more ransom. Now I'm a hostage too."

"He can't mean for you to stay with us!" exclaimed the queen.

"Mother, we have no control over the matter," Julnie pointed out. "I hope he does stay here so he can tell me about Exitorn. I get so bored."

The queen sighed. "There's no use pretending I have any power. Vashton makes all the decisions—even whether we live or die."

"Mother, don't talk like that. Uncle Vashton

wouldn't dare kill us."

"Your uncle has always been hungry for power. Now that he has it, no one is safe." She looked at Brill. "If he said you were to stay here, this is where you'll be. You can sleep on the floor in the sitting room. We'll gather up extra pillows for you."

"That will be fine," said Brill. At least he hadn't been thrown into a dungeon.

Julnie sat down on a small couch and patted the seat next to her. "Sit beside me and tell me about Exitorn."

Brill sat down and told how Julnie's grandfather, King Talder, had regained his throne from the cruel Emperor Immane. When King Talder died from the plague, her Uncle Silgar became king.

Queen Herla said, "We have had a few letters, but it's nice to hear details. I wish I could have seen Father once more." She wiped her eyes again. "Choner was a good king, a lot like Father." She lowered her voice. "A soldier actually killed Choner, but I know Vashton planned it."

"Uncle Vashton said he was locking us in our rooms for our protection, but he's the only one we need protection from," added Julnie.

"I suppose Vashton was afraid I might rally some of Choner's friends to fight against him," continued Queen Herla. "But there was no chance of that. Choner's supporters are hiding."

Julnie got up and walked toward her mother. "Some day Trant will get the throne away from Vashton, Mother."

"Well . . . I just want him safe." Herla went back in her room and shut the door.

Brill walked around, studying his prison. The two narrow windows were only about eight inches wide—too narrow for a person to squeeze through. "I wish the windows were wider," he muttered.

"All the castle windows are narrow—to make it harder for enemy soldiers to shoot arrows through them," explained Julnie. "Are you looking for a way to escape?"

"Of course." Brill tried pushing the stones between the windows, but they wouldn't budge.

"But even if we got out, the soldiers would never let us walk through the gate in the outer wall," pointed out Julnie. "Well, I'm going to change my dress for dinner. Mother says even though we're prisoners and eat our dinner on trays, we're still royal and should act like it."

Brill said, "I don't have any other clothes. My things are in saddlebags at the cathedral stables."

"That's all right. I like your blue tunic."

When Julnie came from her room a little later, she wore a lace-trimmed gown of cream silk.

"You look beautiful," exclaimed Brill, "as if you're going to an important party."

She smiled with pleasure. "I'm celebrating because you're here." She sat beside Brill and fingered a heart-shaped gold locket* hanging around her neck. "Mother and Father gave me this on my fourteenth birthday three months ago. We were so happy then." She opened the locket to show Brill a small hand-painted picture of her father.

At that point a serving girl entered with dinner trays which she placed on a heavy oak table at the side of the room.

Brill pulled out chairs for the queen and Julnie. He

bumped his knee on one of the thick table legs as he slipped into his own seat. He was glad no one commented.

"Better than your usual prison fare," he said as he cut a piece of roast beef.

"How do you know?" Julnie spread honey on a slice of wheat bread.

Brill told of his experiences in the Exitorn dungeon and in the Magran jail.

The queen frowned. "It sounds as if you get into a lot of trouble."

Brill grinned and looked at Julnie. "It's mostly because of your cousin Segra. You'll like her. She's kind and brave and a lot of fun."

Julnie didn't comment.

That night Queen Herla helped Brill put together a bed with pillows and blankets. As he lay awake, he wondered what Segra was doing. Would she worry when Grossder returned to ask for more ransom?

The next few days passed in the same way as the first. One day Brill studied the door lock, trying to think what he could use as a substitute key. "Do you have a nail file I can borrow?" he asked.

Julnie scowled. "Brill, it won't do any good to open the door. Soldiers guard our door."

"Maybe they go away at night."

"I don't think so."

"But I can't stand just waiting."

"I hate it too. But Mother says if they catch us trying to escape, Uncle Vashton will put us in the dungeon where it's all dark and rats run around. I can't stand to think about it."

Brill sighed. If only he could think of some way to

outwit King Vashton.

One day Julnie asked him to tell them more of the adventures he had shared with Segra.

Queen Herla was fascinated with his stories of Stargull. "I'd like to see that remarkable bird," she said.

"When you come to Exitorn, you'll see him. He often flies to the castle tower to see Segra and me."

One afternoon at the end of a week, Brill watched Puffire through one of the narrow windows of the sitting room. The mountain's snow had turned dark gray from the ash. A plume of smoke spurted from the top.

"I'd like to know what's going on inside that mountain." Brill peered at the dingy peak.

He stepped aside as Julnie walked to look out the opening. "A long time ago our city was destroyed by that volcano," she said in a low voice. "I asked Father why they built it back in the same place. He said it's a good place for a city and Puffire sleeps most of the time."

The next morning the shaking floor awoke Brill. He jumped up and ran to the window. A column of smoke was rising from Puffire into a darkening sky. Then with a deafening roar, part of the mountain exploded before his eyes into dark boiling clouds. The palace shook.

"Julnie, it's the volcano!" screamed Brill.

Julnie ran from her room in her gown. Lightning flashed in the mushrooming cloud as it grew to block the sun. She started screaming and clutching at him.

They heard a shout from the corridor outside their room. "Let's get out of here!"

Brill pulled away from Julnie and ran to the door. It was still locked. He shook the latch and yelled, "Open the door! Please open!"

There was no answer.

The queen rushed from her room with a cloak thrown over her nightgown. "What's happening?" she cried.

"The volcano is erupting!" answered Brill.

Julnie finally stopped screaming and looked out the window. "People are fleeing from the castle."

The queen ran to the door and pounded it with her fists. "Let us out!" she shrieked.

Brill dashed back to the window.

Julnie put out her arms and looked at him with fear-glazed eyes. "It's getting dark. What's going to happen to us?"

Brill swallowed. "I don't know. There's no one to open our door."

As the boiling black cloud of ash moved around the castle, Julnie shrieked, "It's turning to night outside!"

The queen wailed.

Brill tried to organize his thoughts. *We have to get out! No, maybe we'd better stay here.* He couldn't make up his mind. He didn't want to join the shadowy people rushing about outside the window, but he felt helpless in his prison.

Finally he said, "If we can get out, we'll need something to cover our noses and mouths so we don't breathe so much ash."

Queen Herla went to her room and returned with silk scarves for each of them.

She stopped at a chair. "That awful dust is seeping into our room. It's all over Choner's favorite chair." Herla tried to brush the ash off the gold upholstery with her hand.

Suddenly the floor shook as another earthquake hit

the city. An ominous roar filled the air.

"The castle! It's falling!" cried the queen.

Brill looked up to see a wall of stones crumbling and the heavy timbered roof sagging above their heads. "Look out," he screamed. "The roof's coming down!"

egra climbed the tallest tower in the castle of Exitorn. She scanned the people dotting the road leading from the capital city. They were too far away to recognize, but she looked for brown curly hair like Brill's. He had been gone almost a month, and an uneasy knot of worry was growing in Segra's mind.

"He'll come back today," she told herself. "He must have paid the ransom by now so my aunt and cousin could go free."

She looked up, squinting against the summer sunlight. Why hadn't Stargull come back? Two weeks earlier she had asked him to check on Brill, and she had expected him to return with a note. He could travel much faster than horses.

She turned as she heard Rima's voice. "Segra, your father wants to see you." Rima stood on the stairs with only her head and shoulders showing.

"What does he want?"

"He didn't say."

Segra looked at Rima. "What's wrong? You're not telling me something."

"We mustn't keep the king waiting."

As Segra followed her lady-in-waiting down the circular staircase, prickles of fear ran up her back. She could tell by Rima's expression that bad news was waiting.

In the throne room, a bedraggled gray figure sat between the king and queen, drinking apple juice.

"Who's the beggar?" whispered Segra to Rima.

Before Rima could answer, King Silgar said, "Segra, come hear this story."

As Segra approached, she cried out with sudden recognition, "Grossder, is that you?"

The gray figure answered, "Yes, Your Highness. I came straight to the castle without washing or changing my clothes."

"What's happened to Brill?" Segra tried to keep her voice steady, but her throat suddenly felt tight, as if she weren't getting enough air.

"There's been a volcanic eruption," said her father. He nodded toward Grossder. "Start at the beginning and tell us your story."

Grossder hesitated a moment as if deciding where to begin. "We went to see King Vashton, but he refused to release the queen and her daughter. He said he wanted bigger jewels, and he sent me back for them."

Trant, who sat near the king, scowled. "I was afraid Uncle Vashton would be hard to deal with. All he cares about is himself."

"Where's Brill?" Impatience gave Segra's voice a shrill tone.

"King Vashton kept him as a hostage to wait for bigger jewels," answered Grossder.

"Then we must send more ransom," cried Segra.

"Let him finish his story," said the king.

"I left the palace, got on my horse, and headed for home," continued Grossder. "On the second night I stopped at the monastery. I was sick. The monks insisted I stay in bed until I felt better. I hated to take their terrible-tasting medicine, but it cured me. In a few days I was ready to travel again. On the morning I was to leave, Monastery Mountain began to shake. We all rushed outside and saw a huge, gray cloud rising from Puffire Volcano. The cloud kept boiling bigger and bigger, and soon we were caught in swirling ash. Father Mekdell said, 'This is the big one. I fear for Yolben. It was destroyed once by Puffire.'

"We didn't know what to do—stay outside and breathe that awful ash or go inside and risk having the monastery fall on us. We finally went into the chapel to pray for all the people near the volcano."

Segra interrupted again. "Do you know what happened to Brill?"

"I'm getting to that. By the next day the ash had quit blowing around so much, so I headed back to Yolben. The road was gone, and whole forests were lying on the ground apparently knocked down by the volcano's blast. I could see a huge avalanche* where a big part of the mountain had slid into the valley below. Some places were still smoking with fires. I got off my horse and led her so I could watch for hot spots."

"Did you get back to Yolben?" asked Trant.

Grossder's voice broke. "There wasn't much left of the city. Houses had collapsed and burned, and everything was half buried in ash."

"Were any people alive?" The queen spoke slowly, her voice filled with concern.

"Not that I could see."

"What about the castle?" exclaimed Trant.

"It was a pile of blackened stones buried in ash. Prisoners wouldn't have had a chance."

Trant jumped up. "I must go back to look for my mother and sister."

Segra's eyes filled with tears. "Poor Brill! Let me go too, Father!"

King Silgar put out his arms toward his daughter and held her. He looked at Grossder. "Could anyone have escaped?"

"I found people who had moved farther south. A couple of them were palace servants. They thought King Vashton had been killed because no one had seen him since the eruption."

"Did you ask about Queen Herla and Julnie?" asked the king.

"Yes, but no one had seen them either. The servant said they were locked in their rooms, so they couldn't have escaped before the palace collapsed."

"What about Brill?" Segra wiped her eyes.

"I asked, but no one had heard of him. People were mourning for their own family members and worrying about finding food, so they didn't pay much attention to me."

"Vashton will not be missed." Trant clenched his fists.

"Who will rule now?" asked the king.

"My cousin Kadbar if he's still alive—unless I can rally forces and take over."

"What kind of a king would Kadbar make?"

Trant scowled. "Probably worse than his father. He's mean and selfish."

"I'll send soldiers to search for Brill, Herla, and Julnie," said King Silgar.

Queen Nalane added, "I'll order servants to gather food and clothing for the survivors. The soldiers can deliver them."

Trant bowed. "Thank you, Your Majesty. I would like to go with your soldiers, if I may." His voice shook. "I must find the truth and see how I can help my country."

The king nodded, then turned to Grossder. "Thank you for your bravery in a dangerous mission. But Segra—" he put his hands on her shoulders—"you must not go. You know that."

Segra nodded and walked away. She went slowly up the countless stairs of the tower to scan the skies for Stargull. She couldn't believe Brill was dead. Stargull would find him and bring her word . . . but the large, white bird didn't come.

Mud Bath 6

he floor shook and another wall collapsed.

"Get under the table," screamed Brill.

Queen Herla, Julnie, and Brill scrambled under the heavy oak table as the timbered roof crashed down. The table kept the roof from crushing them. The timbers rested on the rubble of stones from the fallen walls.

Brill looked out and said, "I think we can crawl out under the roof."

"What if there's another earthquake?" asked Julnie, pushing closer to him.

"That's why we better go quickly before it comes,"

he answered. "Do you want me to lead, Queen Herla?"

"Go ahead," answered the queen. She looked at her daughter. "We must be brave, Julnie. You go next."

Brill crawled along in the space two feet high between the floor and the collapsed roof. As he moved a broken chair out of the way, a timber slipped lower, and he held his breath, hoping it wasn't all coming down. The unstable roof hung just above their heads.

As Brill came closer to the end of the room, there was even less space. A pile of stones from the fallen wall blocked his way. Brill felt despair. Had he led them to a dead end? Should they have stayed under the table and hoped for rescue?

"Brill, I smell something burning!" cried Julnie. "What is it?"

"I don't know." But shivers of fear ran up Brill's back. The castle timbers must be on fire!

"How do we get out?" demanded Julnie.

"I'm looking for a way," he answered. He lay on his stomach and squirmed under the small space by the fallen stones. He saw a place where two large stones a foot apart held the roof timbers a little higher. "I see a hole between two stones. Keep following," he called back to Julnie and the queen.

Brill squeezed between the rocks. Suddenly he felt a breeze. "I'm out," he called back, choking on thick ash swirling around him. He guided Julnie and then her mother through the small opening.

Julnie stood and stared at the castle rubble. Brill pulled her away just in time from the stones and wood still clattering down.

"Oh, no!" cried the queen. "The castle's on fire! The poor people!"

Brill felt his stomach twist in a painful knot as he stared at the flames dotting the castle ruins in several places. The smell of smoke mingled with the rotten egg smell from the sulfur* of the volcano.

"Is the whole city burning?" gasped Julnie. It was hard to tell what was smoke and what was ash. The city was veiled in a strange, dark fog.

They each silently tied one of the queen's scarves over their faces below their eyes, hoping to filter out some of the gray ash. It was fine like bath powder and as thick as a snow blizzard.

Julnie blinked. "My eyes hurt! That dust stings."

"Let's go to the river," suggested the queen. "It might be better on the other side." She led the way over the stones that had been the outer castle wall.

As they passed a stooped figure, Herla stopped. "Ulfa! Is that you?"

"Oh, Your Majesty." The old woman bowed to the queen. "I'm so glad you're safe."

Herla put her hand on Ulfa's shoulder. "Come with us. We're going across the river."

"I can't walk very fast."

"We'll go at your pace." Herla turned to Brill. "Ulfa was my faithful servant for many years."

"Hello, Ulfa," he said, then turned to the queen. "I want to find my horse if I can. I left her at the cathedral stable." Brill shuddered as he thought of the destruction around him. What had happened to Comet?

"We could use a horse," said Herla. "Julnie, go with Brill. You can show him the way to the river. We'll meet on the other side of the bridge. Be careful."

Julnie frowned. "It's getting darker and darker. How can we find our way?"

"Go slowly. You know the city well," said the queen. She took the frail old woman's arm. "Come, Ulfa. I'll help you."

Brill and Julnie walked with their heads bent to keep from breathing in the ash, which seeped through their scarves. As they stepped over the debris,* snatches of conversation drifted toward them.

"Tula, where are you? Please come to Mother!"

"Water! Get water from the river to put out the fire."

"Rosna, we can't save our things. We have to get out of here!"

The wooden houses they passed had collapsed like tents in a gale. The gray ash began to mix with perspiration, forming an uncomfortable paste on Brill's skin. He felt Julnie grip his hand.

"I have my eyes closed," she whispered. "I can't stand the dust in my eyes."

"Open them, Julnie, or you'll fall. There's rubble everywhere."

Julnie opened her eyes and screamed. "Eek! A dead body! I almost stepped on it."

Brill's stomach twisted the knot harder, and he looked away. "That's why you have to watch where you're going."

"O Brill, I can't stand this! Our city ruined. People dead! I wish Mother had stayed with us." She began to sob.

"It is terrible, but we're alive, and we have to go on," Brill said softly.

When they reached the cathedral, they found that it too was a mass of rubble. They picked their way around the jumble of stones and wood to the stable. Brill blinked back tears as he saw that the roof had collapsed.

"Poor Comet! I hope someone let out the horses before the roof collapsed." He looked at Julnie. "We'll have to walk."

"How far must we go to get out of this awful dust?" she asked.

"I wish I knew. God has kept us alive so far. He won't desert us now."

Brill and Julnie stumbled along with other shadowy figures trying to escape the thick ash.

They trudged through the foot-deep layer of ash without talking. The scarves they wore over their mouths and noses were now gray.

They climbed over rubble that had been the city wall. "The river's this way," said Julnie.

That was the direction away from the road that led to Exitorn. Would he ever get back to Segra? Brill wondered.

"Julnie, is that you?" called a woman's weak voice from up ahead.

"Yes, Ulfa." Julnie stopped. "Where's Mother?"

"They took her," gasped Ulfa.

"What do you mean?" cried Julnie.

"We were walking along, and soldiers grabbed her. One said, 'We've found the queen!' "

"Were they Vashton's men?" asked Brill.

"I suppose so. I didn't recognize them. They had masks over their faces like you do." Her voice broke. "I'd give my life for the queen, but I couldn't fight half a dozen men."

Julnie turned to Brill. "We have to find Mother!"

Ulfa shook her head. "They were on horses, Your Highness. You could never catch them."

Brill looked at the princess. "I'm sorry, Julnie. Which direction did they go, Ulfa?"

"This way," Ulfa pointed. "I think. But they could have changed direction."

"I wish I had never left Mother," Julnie moaned.

"Don't blame yourself," Ulfa comforted. "I'm glad they didn't catch you too." She looked at Brill. "Please keep the princess safe. And don't wait for me."

"But you need help," Julnie protested as she took Ulfa's arm.

"No, Julnie. I've decided to head south, where my daughter lives." She pulled away. "May God bless you."

Julnie said, "God bless you too, Ulfa." They watched her leave.

"Are we close to the river?" asked Brill.

"It's down this hill," said Julnie.

They groped their way through an ash-covered forest. Brill tried to cough up the ash that clogged his throat.

As they came to the end of the trees, Julnie pointed. "There's the river."

Brill walked to it, longing to splash water on his ash-covered face and hands. But as he looked down at the gray water, he grumbled, "The river is full of ash too."

Julnie sighed. "This gray world must be a nightmare. I hope I wake up soon."

Kneeling, Brill ran his hand in the ashy water. "It's warm," he said.

"Of course. Everything's mixed up in dreams."

Brill hoped Julnie was only pretending. She couldn't really think this was only a bad dream. He stood. "Which way's the bridge?"

"It's downstream—not very far. You could see it if the ash wasn't so thick."

"Maybe the air will be better on the other side." He began walking.

Suddenly Julnie screamed. "Brill, watch out!"

Brill looked upstream. A ten-foot high wall of mud rushed toward them. Before they could run, a muddy, hot river, carrying logs, parts of houses, and dead fish swept them downstream. The rushing water overflowed the banks, widening the river to three times its normal size.

Brill grabbed onto a bucking log and clung to a piece of branch. He pulled himself onto the log and looked for Julnie, but he couldn't see her. "Julnie," he cried. "Where are you?" She didn't answer. He hoped she had not been sucked under the floating logs into the scorching water.

With an impact that almost unbalanced him, his log suddenly crashed into a pile of logs which had formed behind the bridge. Another fallen tree hit his leg. He scrambled up on the log jam, jumping from one log to another to keep out of the way of debris which rammed into it. He wanted to hurry across to reach the other side of the river, but he had to find Julnie first. He called again, "Julnie! Please answer me."

He heard a faint *"Help! Help me!"*

Scrambling toward the sound, he saw Julnie's mud-colored hair and her arm around a log. He bounded over the logs toward her. *Lord, help me rescue Julnie,* he prayed as he saw her arm lose its grip. She slipped into the thick, hot river and disappeared.

"Julnie!" screamed Brill. He straddled the log where she had gone down. She bobbed to the surface. He grabbed hold of her long hair and hung on. Julnie reached up her hand, and he clutched it, pulling with all his might until at last she slid onto the growing pile of logs.

She coughed and sputtered and tried to wipe the thick gray paste from her face. Her scarf, thick with mud, still covered her mouth and nose. She pushed it off so it hung around her neck. "Can't see," she choked.

Brill tried to wipe mud from her eyelashes with his fingers and scarf. "We have to get out of here before the bridge collapses," he warned.

"My leg hurts. I can't walk," she groaned.

"But we must get to the other side of the river. We don't want to get buried in another mudflow."

"I told you. I can't walk. I think my leg is broken."

"Then I'll carry you." He picked her up. Julnie put her arms around his neck and hung on. Though she was not heavy, carrying her made it harder to keep his balance. He panted in the dusty air as he stepped from log to log. One log rolled as he put his foot on it, and they slipped into the muddy water up to Brill's nose.

Julnie struggled, but Brill kept one arm around her and grabbed a log with the other. He boosted her up on the log. "We'll make it," he gasped, joining her.

"Go without me," said Julnie. "I'm too heavy for you."

He shook his head. "I won't leave you."

When he had carried her over the pile of logs, he stepped off into thick, knee-high mud. "We made it," he exclaimed. They looked back just in time to see the bridge give way and the logjam rush downstream.

"Thank you, Brill," whispered Julnie. "You're very brave."

"How does your leg feel?"

"It hurts a lot. O Brill, what's going to happen to us?"

"We'll survive." Brill tried to sound confident for Julnie's sake. He pushed his way through the mud, which grew shallower as he neared solid ground. The ash was not falling as thickly now, so he could see a little farther. "We're coming to higher ground. We'll soon be out of this mud."

Beyond the mud, more tree trunks lay on the ground. A few still stood, but they looked dead.

"Why did the trees fall?" asked Julnie.

Brill shrugged. "I don't know exactly. Maybe when the volcano exploded, the hot gas blew them down."

"It looks as if a giant pushed them over."

A bloodcurdling cry sent a shiver up Brill's spine.

"What's that?" cried Julnie.

"Somebody's in pain," said Brill.

"Maybe it's the giant!"

"Julnie! There isn't really a giant."

"But it sounds like some sort of monster." Julnie looked at him with eyes wide with fear.

* * * * *

Almost a month passed before the soldiers returned from their mission to Brislan. Segra hurried to the throne room to hear their news.

The leader reported, "Towns close to the volcano were completely buried by the huge avalanche. Yolben was somewhat protected from the hot blast of the explosion by the high hill to the north of it."

"Then why did the houses fall down?" asked Segra.

"The survivors said a lot of their damage came from the earthquakes. To the south of Yolben, many towns are still standing. People are trying to shovel the ash away from their homes and fields, but it's hard to get rid of it."

"We traveled throughout Brislan's countryside to question people," added another soldier. "They were eager to talk when we gave them food and clothes."

"Did Trant stay with you?" asked King Silgar.

"No, he left us when we reached Brislan, so he could look for his friends. He said it would be dangerous for us if Kadbar's men saw us together. We might all end up in prison."

"Did you ask everyone if they had seen Brill?" asked Segra.

"Yes, Your Highness," answered the leader. "We found one of the men who guarded the door to Queen Herla's rooms where Brill was. He said the door was always locked from the outside."

"Why didn't they unlock the door on the day of the eruption?" asked the king.

"He said that would have been against their orders. He and the other guard ran when they felt the first strong earthquake. They looked back and saw the castle crumble. He assured me no one could have gotten out alive. Even if by some miracle they had, they probably would have died outside."

The wind of despair blew out the tiny flicker of hope Segra had kept lit during the long weeks of waiting.

"We will have a memorial service for Duke Brill at the cathedral," said the king.

Segra nodded and hurried to her room. She wanted

to be alone where tears could relieve some of the painful pressure building in her aching heart.

* * * * *

As Segra marched down the cathedral aisle to take her place at Brill's memorial service, she tried to freeze her emotions and stop her brain from remembering. Princesses were to be calm, and she wanted to hold her tears until she was alone again.

King Yardo, Queen Sera, and Prince Oplack of Leoniff attended the service. "Brill was a brave young man," said King Yardo to the assembled crowd. "He helped save my kingdom when it had been taken over by the evil Chief Umber."

King Silgar too recounted Brill's brave deeds. "He risked his life to help King Talder regain his throne, and he rescued me from the King of Magra. He helped stop the war between Exitorn and Chief Umber, and he searched for the Zinders so their medicine could cure plague victims. In doing so, he saved my life as I was dying of the plague."

Then the bishop spoke and read Bible passages explaining God's promise of a life that never ends for those who have accepted Christ's gift of forgiveness for their sins.

Segra thought of Brill living in heaven with no more troubles or worries, and she felt a little comforted. Some day she'd see him again. He would enjoy showing heaven to her.

After the service, Prince Oplack took Segra's hand. "I will miss Brill very much," he said. "I know you feel even worse, and I wish I could do something to make your hurt go away."

"Thanks, Oplack." She gently pulled her hand away.

They returned to the palace, and Segra again slipped away to climb the tower. Through tear-glazed eyes, she searched the skies for Stargull. Why hadn't he returned? Had he been caught in the eruption?

rill listened as the howl came again. He had heard a similar cry before.

"It's a monster!" Julnie cried.

"No, it's not, Julnie. It sounds like a dragator.*"

"A dragator! Hurry! I don't want a dragator to eat us."

Brill laughed. "We don't look very appetizing, all covered with gray mud."

"Don't joke at a time like this," scolded Julnie.

"Dragators are kind," said Brill. "When we have time, I'll tell you how they've helped Segra and me."

The next howl was louder.

"Look! There he is," cried Julnie. "Run!"

But Brill carried her nearer to the dragon-like beast.

Julnie screamed, "Brill! Don't go any closer!"

Brill saw that one of the dragator's feet was caught in a small logjam. He was squirming frantically, trying to free his foot, but it was stuck fast.

"Poor dragator," Brill said as he stopped several yards away.

Julnie sniffed. "I don't feel sorry for him. I've seen too many dead people today to waste any sympathy on a dragator."

"Dragators are smart. They suffer just like we do."

"They're ugly and they scare me," insisted Julnie. "Oh, I wish I had stayed with Mother." The dragator looked at Julnie, and howled again.

"Brill, let's go!"

Brill sighed, then carried Julnie out of the mud and put her down on an ash-covered mound.

The plaintive cry of the dragator pierced Brill's thoughts. He argued with himself.

I must help that poor dragator.

What could you do? The log's too big to lift.

I have to try.

You don't want to go back in that awful mud.

No, I don't, but I can't just walk away from a dragator in trouble. They've saved my life more than once.

Brill stood. "I'm going back to see if I can help the dragator."

"Don't leave me."

"I'll be right back."

"He might eat you!"

"He'll know I'm trying to help him."

"But I'm scared to be alone." Julnie looked at him with pleading brown eyes. "What if another mudflow comes along? I can't run out of the way with my broken leg."

"I'll run back if I see trouble coming," promised Brill. He plop-plopped through the slow-moving mud toward the howls. The mud grew deeper with each step until it was almost to his knees.

As he came to the dragator, he spoke softly. "I'll try to set you free." Brill grabbed the end of the log that pinned down the animal's foot and tried with all his strength to lift it. It wouldn't budge.

"That's heavy," he gasped.

The dragator bellowed as if to agree.

"I'll be right back." Brill waded through the mud, looking for the right-sized pole among the pieces of wood washed down with the mudflow. He found the trunk of a sapling and returned to the dragator. "I'm going to push the log up. Pull your leg out as soon as you can."

Brill wedged his pole under the log and after several tries managed to raise the log a few inches.

The dragator pulled his foot out and bellowed his thanks. The beast limped away, and Brill returned to Julnie.

"Where are we going now?" she asked.

"We'll keep going until we get out of this ash." He lifted Julnie and started across the fallen forest. Sometimes he stepped over the logs, and sometimes he walked on them. Wisps of smoke curled up from underground pockets of fire, which had been started by lightning and kept smoldering even under the ash.

"I wish they hadn't built our city so close to Puffire," said Julnie.

"Maybe they'll rebuild in a safer place."

Julnie sighed. "It won't be my city anymore with Vashton ruling."

"Do you think your brother Trant could rally enough men to overthrow Vashton?"

"I know a lot of men in Brislan are still loyal to my father, but I don't know if there are enough."

Brill yawned. "It must be getting close to night."

"It's been night since this morning."

"I know. It's kind of a twilight now, but I don't have any idea what time it really is," said Brill.

"It seems as if we've been in this nightmare forever."

"I sure am hungry. We didn't even have breakfast."

"I'm more thirsty than hungry," said Julnie. "I wish we'd find a nice cool, clean stream."

Brill lowered Julnie to a log and sat down to rest. "Is your leg any better?"

"No. It feels as if someone's sticking needles in it."

"Maybe I could put splints on it. I watched Segra put splints on my friend Grossder's arm once."

Brill found two branches he could use as splints. He cut them the right size with the knife he wore on his belt. He tore his scarf into strips, shaking off as much ash as he could.

He knelt beside Julnie. "Show me where it hurts."

She pulled her skirt up a bit and pointed to the calf area. "Right there."

Brill felt it gently. "Nothing seems to be out of place."

"It sure hurts," she insisted.

"Of course. But it would be worse if the bones had come apart."

"How do you know so much?"

He shrugged. He didn't want to admit how little he did know.

He tied on the splints.

"That feels better. I won't have to worry so much about bumping it. Thanks, Brill."

Brill picked up Julnie and prayed as he walked. *God, help me to know which way to go. We need food, water, and fresh air. Lord, lead us out of this awful ash. And please take care of Queen Herla.*

He tried to walk faster. "This is like walking on a beach, only the ash doesn't stay on the ground like beach sand."

"I've never been to a beach. I don't think I'd like it," said Julnie.

"Beaches are fun. The sand doesn't blow into your eyes and noses and ears like this ash. When you come to Exitorn, I'll take you to the seashore."

He looked at Julnie. Suddenly, he stepped off a large log and his foot sank down. He had fallen into a hidden fire, and it was burning through his worn leather boot. He screamed, and Julnie lunged out of his arms onto a log.

Free of the load, Brill pulled up his flaming boot and dropped to the ground, scooping up handfuls of ash in a desperate attempt to smother the flames now licking his hose.

"Brill!" Julnie screamed.

Brill felt faint, and he lay down, fighting to stay conscious. Everything seemed to spin around—everything except his throbbing foot.

"Is there anything I can do?" Julnie's tearful voice seemed far away. "Brill, please answer me."

* * * * *

Segra looked out through a low place in the battlements.* Below lay the capital city and beyond it the countryside of farms, small villages, and patches of forest. She felt a wave of tenderness. This was where her people lived.

I will never love anyone in the same way I have loved Brill, she thought. *Now that he's gone I should devote myself to my country. God made me a princess, and one day I'll be queen. I must stop thinking of myself and my sorrow and follow God's calling.*

But the ache in her heart wouldn't go away, and she continued to cry herself to sleep for many nights.

One day she approached her father. "Father, I know it is time for me to marry. I am willing to marry Prince Oplack if you still think this is best for Exitorn."

King Silgar spoke solemnly. "Are you sure, Segra?"

"Yes, Father. I feel God wants me to do what is right for my country."

"King Yardo asked me about it again when he was here," her father said, stroking his chin. "He and I feel that a strong alliance between us is the best way to protect our countries from the King of Magra to the north and from the wily* chieftains of Asperita to the south."

"I understand," said Segra.

"I will write King Yardo the good news, and we'll set the date. You and your mother can begin making wedding plans." He kissed her forehead.

Segra left to find her mother. Somehow she'd hoped that doing the right thing would make the empty feeling in her heart go away . . . but it was still there.

Help! Help! 8

 rill! Brill! Answer me." Julnie's voice finally awoke Brill from unconsciousness.

He slowly sat up and uncovered his foot. Clumps of ash clung to the raw, red flesh.

"The fire's out," he breathed. "I'll be all right. I just need to rest awhile." He fell back. But his foot still felt as if flames were licking it. He forced himself to sit up to take another look. Only the upper half of his boot remained. He tried to remove it, but the scorched leather stuck to his skin. His foot was blistered and black, and he couldn't tell which was his skin and which was ash coating.

"How will you walk with no sole on your boot?" Julnie cried.

"I'll manage." He curled up on the ashy ground. Closing his eyes, he imagined he was back in Exitorn, far away from pain and ashy air. He was sitting down in the castle dining hall to a meal of roast beef, carrots, rolls, and fruit. The picture made his stomach grumble. He concentrated on Segra. Would she worry about him when Grossder came back alone? He didn't want her to worry, but he didn't like to think that she might not care either.

Julnie's voice brought him back to the present. "Can you walk?"

"Of course. I just thought we needed to rest." He tried not to let Julnie see how much pain he felt. If he couldn't walk, what would they do? Sit and starve in this fallen forest? Brill felt beaten. With both of them injured, what hope was there?

After resting awhile, Brill stood. But as the blood rushed to his burned foot, the intense pain made him quickly sit down.

Julnie frowned. "You can't walk!"

"I'll have to rest a little longer." He looked around at the gray ground and gray air. He longed to see a green plant or a blue stream—anything that wasn't gray. He saw no people. Perhaps no one else from Yolben had crossed the river.

They sat in silence until Julnie said, "I'm thirsty. I need to wash this ash out of my throat."

"Me too. Somewhere we'll find a stream of cool water."

"But we don't know how far we'll have to walk to find an unspoiled forest. We may die of thirst long before that." Tears cut lines in Julnie's mask of mud.

"We'll make it. I know we will," declared Brill—with much more confidence than he felt. Oh, how he missed Segra. But he knew it would take time for his foot to heal. There was no way he could stand the terrible pain of walking—not even to go to her . . . and not even to escape death.

Julnie started sobbing loudly. "It would have been better if the roof had collapsed on us. Then the end would have been quick."

"Don't talk like that. God is leading us. He won't desert us now after bringing us this far."

Julnie wiped her eyes on her damp sleeve. "I hate having no water or food. Brill, we've got to get out of here. See if you can walk yet."

He shook his head. "I can't."

"At least try."

"My foot throbs even when I don't put weight on it. Maybe by tomorrow . . . "

"We'll need water before then," Julnie cried.

"Pray, Julnie. Pray that God will send someone to help."

Julnie sniffled. "There's no one around to send. We're all alone, and neither one of us can walk."

Brill wished Segra was with him instead of Julnie. Segra wouldn't whine like this. But then he chided himself for the selfish thought. He was glad Segra was safe in the Exitorn palace. But would he ever see her again? And would she know what had happened to him?

"My leg hurts," complained Julnie.

"And my foot burns, but it doesn't do any good to complain," snapped Brill. "Maybe I can crawl to look for water."

"No! Don't leave me! You'll never find me again in all this ash."

But I wouldn't have to listen to your whining, thought Brill.

They were silent. Then Julnie suggested, "Maybe you could make crutches."

"I couldn't carry you and walk with crutches."

"You'd have to make crutches for both of us."

Brill thought a moment. "It's worth trying." He slowly began to crawl around and dig in the ash for tree branches or small trunks. Finding forked sticks the right size wouldn't be easy, but at least it gave him something to do.

Julnie scratched in the ash around her.

"Be careful of hot spots," he warned her.

A little later she called, "Find anything?"

"Not yet."

"Don't go too far away."

"I'm not very far." Any branches or small trunks which were strong enough to hold a person's weight were too long. He returned to Julnie.

"I can't find anything suitable to use for a crutch," he reported. "With my knife it would take forever to whittle one of these trunks down to the right length."

"I didn't find anything either." said Julnie.

Brill sat still for a minute, resting his foot. Then he sat up. "Let's try calling for help."

"All right. Maybe there *is* someone out there." She yelled, "Help! HELP!" as loud as she could.

Brill added his voice. "Help! Help us!"

Julnie suddenly stopped and coughed. "I swallowed more ash," she said hoarsely.

"Put your hand over your mouth."

She gave a muffled shout.

Brill leaned wearily against a fallen log and looked up at the gray sky. He suspected that even if they were heard, no one would rush to their rescue. Everyone was fighting for survival. No one would be likely to dash across the ash desert to investigate cries for help.

All at once Julnie screamed, "Brill! Help!"

"What's the matter?"

"A dragator's coming!" she shrieked.

"Julnie, that's great! Thank God!" The dragator Brill had rescued was lumbering toward them. "Hey, dragator," Brill called. "Come here. We need your help."

The dragator hurried to him.

"We can't walk," explained Brill. "Can we ride on your back to find water?"

The dragator bellowed as if to echo Brill's need for water. He knelt beside Brill, folding his legs under his scaly body, and Brill climbed onto his bumpy back. He tried to find a comfortable spot between the bony triangular plates.

"I'm sorry Julnie screamed when she saw you," Brill quietly said. "She's not used to dragators."

"Climb aboard," Brill called down to Julnie. "We're going to look for water."

Julnie's eyes widened. "What if he eats us?"

"Julnie! If you talk like that, he'll leave."

Julnie gingerly struggled on, then clung to Brill's waist.

"We're ready," said Brill.

The dragator stood up and lumbered off. Soon they were going up, heading for what looked like a pass between the mountains.

"Maybe the air will get better higher up," said Brill.

"I hope so."

"If Segra were here, she'd give the dragator a name. How about Samaritan? Remember how the good Samaritan rescued the man who had been hurt?"

"Seems like a funny name for such a scary-looking creature, but I guess it sort of fits."

On the other side of the high ridge, trees still stood. Apparently the chain of peaks had protected the valley below from the full force of the volcanic explosion. Ash covered everything, but as Samaritan descended between the trees, the air grew clearer.

"I can breathe better," cried Julnie.

"Look, plants are growing under the trees," pointed out Brill. "Maybe we can eat some—if we shake off the ash."

"But how will we know which ones are safe to eat?"

"Blackberries and huckleberries would be all right," answered Brill. But he realized that finding food in the forest would be risky when he didn't know much about plants.

At the bottom of the valley floor, they came to a stream somewhat gray from ash, but much clearer than the muddy river. Brill slipped from the dragator's back, putting all his weight on his good foot. Then he helped Julnie down.

Samaritan lay down in the shallow stream and gulped water. Brill and Julnie scooped the cool water up with their hands and drank it. It was a bit ashy, but wonderfully wet.

"Thank you, Samaritan," said Brill. "You saved our lives."

Samaritan bellowed and stood, then tramped downstream.

"I'm glad we found water, even if it is ashy." Julnie looked around at the trees and plants. "How will we find food when neither of us can walk?"

"I can crawl," said Brill.

"We should have had the dragator take us where there were people to help us."

"We couldn't cross that terrible mudflow again. Besides, we had to go where the dragator was going. He wanted to find water, not only to drink, but to live in." Brill put his burnt foot into the cool water and felt some relief. Gradually the water soaked off the parts of his boot and hose that were stuck to his skin, leaving raw sores.

"Is that good for your foot?" asked Julnie.

"I don't know, but it feels better in the cold water."

"What are we going to do next?"

"Stay here until I'm able to walk. At least we won't die of thirst."

Julnie dipped her scarf into the water, and tried to wash some of the mud from her face. "I wish I had a clean cloth and clean water." She took off her locket, washed it in the water, and dried it on her gown.

Then she pulled herself onto a nearby log.

"Get off my log!" cried a muffled voice.

Julnie screeched and stood on her one good leg. "Brill, come quick!"

A head popped out from one end of the partly hollow tree trunk.

"Ashmi!" cried Brill.

The little man crawled out and stretched his small frame up to its full two feet. "How do you know my name?" He put his hands on his hips and glared at Brill.

"I'm Brill from Exitorn. You helped make plague

medicine for us. Remember?"

"You look like a gray ogre* from the caves."

"I'm Brill, and this is Princess Julnie from Brislan."

"What are you doing in Zinder country?" demanded Ashmi.

"Trying to survive the volcano's blast."

"Terrible thing! Worst eruption I've ever seen."

"Yolben was destroyed," explained Brill.

Ashmi scowled. "Slugs and slime! I hope we won't get a bunch of big people tramping through our forest. I hate big people!"

"What have we ever done to you?" demanded Julnie.

"We used to live in Exitorn where people made fun of us because we were small and lived in trees. The people of Magra were even worse—they captured us and kept us penned up so we'd make medicine for them."

"Remember who helped you escape," reminded Brill.

"That was only because you wanted us to help you," grumbled Ashmi.

Brill didn't argue with him. Ashmi was as cantankerous* as ever.

"Where are the rest of your band?" asked Brill.

"Out looking for Ulat. He left yesterday to look for zimba roots. Chela's worried he may have been buried in ash."

"Why aren't you helping?" asked Julnie.

"I figure if he's buried, we'll never find him. If he isn't, he'll come home. Even though he's my father, I don't see any reason to rush around looking for him in all that ash."

"It will be good to see Chela again," said Brill.

Ashmi scowled at him. "Bees and beavers, I hope you aren't planning to stay here. Any time we get mixed up with big people, there's trouble. I suggest you head back to your own land. We don't want you here."

"But we can't walk," cried Julnie.

"What do you mean you can't walk? How'd you get here?" demanded Ashmi.

"We rode on the back of a dragator. He brought us here and then headed downstream," explained Brill.

Ashmi stamped his foot. "This is our home. Hawks and hogs, we don't want big people living with us! That never works!"

Life with the Zinders

s Ashmi bustled about shaking ash from the plants near the stream, Julnie whispered to Brill, "What are we going to do?"

"We'll stay here. Ashmi's not as hard-hearted as he sounds. The other Zinders will help us."

"Will they give us food?"

"It'll be mostly leaves and roots, but it'll keep us alive."

"How about fish and game?"

"The Zinders don't kill animals. They don't cook either."

Julnie wrinkled her nose. "You mean it's raw?"

"The Zinders say it's healthier that way."

"Oh, I wish I had a thick slice of bread spread with honey."

Brill pulled his foot from the cold water. As the numbness wore off, it began to throb again.

Ashmi stomped over to him. "Nasty sore," he commented.

"I stepped into an underground fire."

"What's the matter with her?" Ashmi nodded toward Julnie.

"Broken leg."

"I wish I had been awake when that dragator dumped you. I'd have told him to take you away. Quakes and quails, we have enough trouble feeding ourselves without trying to find food to fill two *big* stomachs."

Julnie's eyes flashed anger. "Why don't you just go away and leave us to die?"

"I might do that. I'm the chief, and I can move my tribe farther downstream."

Brill tried to change the subject. "How's your daughter Chela?"

"She's growing tall—almost two feet now. She's a good nurse and is learning about healing herbs from Tala. But she still has a mind of her own. I told her to gather food, but no, she had to go traipsing around in the ash to look for Ulat."

At that moment Wokper, Gurat, and two other Zinders came through the trees.

"Did you find Ulat?" called Ashmi.

"No, but we found another lost Zinder," answered Gurat, stepping aside so Ashmi could see the boy behind him.

"Zack!" exclaimed Brill.

"Vicious volcano. Made a mess of everything," Zack complained. He looked at Brill. "What are you doing here?"

"Trying to get away from the ash."

Ashmi scowled at Zack. "Another mouth to feed! Who are you?"

"Zack from Orkel's tribe. I was kidnapped by big people, and I'm trying to find my way home."

Wokper said, "He's been telling me news about my old friends."

"Where are the rest of the searchers?" asked Ashmi.

"They stopped to pull up zimba roots," explained Gurat. "Chela went to see why some bird was flapping his wings but not getting off the ground."

Zack walked over to Brill. "What's wrong with your foot?"

"Burned it. This is Princess Julnie."

"Ho, there. What's wrong with you?"

"Broke my leg."

Later, the rest of the Zinders, except for Chela, wandered in tired and discouraged after their long search.

"We've been invaded by a couple of big people who can't walk and expect us to feed them," Ashmi explained.

"We're glad to see you again," whispered Tala. "Don't pay any attention to Ashmi."

Neba, whom Brill had last seen as a toddler, was now a young child. She stared at him. "Why are you so big?"

"I'm one of the big people Ashmi complains about."

Neba backed away, but her mother Tala said, "You don't have to be afraid of Brill, Neba."

Brill looked up to see a large white bird walking to camp on two Zinder legs. He blinked. Stargull! Chela was carrying him.

"Put him down. He's too big for you to carry," cried Brill, wishing he could help. "What happened?"

"His wing is burned and he can't fly," gasped Chela as she placed him gently on the ground. "I wish he could tell me how he got hurt. Perhaps he got hit by lightning." She looked at Brill. "Brill! What happened? Your poor foot!"

Brill repeated his story and introduced Julnie.

Then Chela took dried herbs from a sack she had been carrying and soaked them in water from the stream. She gently packed them on Brill's burned foot and tied them on with vines. "This will relieve the pain and fight infection."

Julnie asked, "Do you have anything that will help me?"

"I don't know what to do for broken bones except keep them still until they grow together again," answered Chela.

"I tried to find sticks to make crutches for us," said Brill, "but I didn't find any the right size."

"I'll ask Wokper," said Chela. "He's very clever at making things."

Meanwhile, Tala washed the zimba roots and sliced them on large grepa leaves. Her husband, Gurat, added blackberries and dandelion leaves.

"I'm starving," said Zack.

"Our food supply is a bit low," apologized Tala.

"In the morning we'll leave," Ashmi grumbled. "We can't take care of big people and birds. Storks and storms, we have to watch out for ourselves."

"Papa, you don't mean that," chided Chela. She brought leaves of food to Brill and Julnie. "You can eat the leaf too," she explained.

"What are we going to do about Ulat?" asked Gurat.

Wokper stroked his white beard. "I don't know where else to look."

"He might be hurt. He'll die if we don't find him," said Chela.

"We have to keep searching," agreed Gurat.

"I'll stay here with Neba and gather food tomorrow," said Tala.

"I'll stay too," said Wokper. "I'm too old to walk as far as we did today."

"I'll help search," declared Zack. "It was scary trying to find my way out of that gray world. I didn't know if anyone was left alive!"

"When we first heard you yelling, we thought it might be Ulat," said Gurat.

"It's not polite to tell me you wish I was Ulat. I can't help who I am."

Brill interrupted. "Gurat, when you're looking for Ulat please keep a lookout for Julnie's mother, Queen Herla."

"Sure, but she's probably not in Zinder country."

Brill chewed the root slices and the leaves for a long time. He ate the sweet blackberries slowly.

Julnie whispered, "I didn't like anything except the berries, and I'm still hungry."

"We'll have to be satisfied with Zinder portions." But Brill wondered if they could survive on such meager rations.

Chela fed Stargull leaves and grass seeds.

Later, when it began to grow dark, Gurat gathered

large branches and leaned them against a big log to form two shelters. "You can sleep in these," he said. "They'll protect you from the wind and cold."

"Thanks." Brill crawled to his shelter, and Julnie scooted over to hers, lifting herself with her arms and good leg as she moved. The Zinders climbed trees for sleeping.

Brill lay awake under his branch canopy and relived the horror of the day, but he could see God's guidance through it all. *Thank You, God, for caring for us. Help Julnie's mother and Ulat and all the other people who are in trouble because of the eruption.* Brill remembered how Ulat had freed Segra and him when Prince Jaspar had left them tied to trees in the Magran forest.

The next morning when Brill awoke, the ash had settled some more. Gurat had already led the small search party away, toward the mountains.

Brill and Julnie rested while Tala and Neba gathered food and Ashmi grumbled. Wokper was working on their crutches. He found two saplings, chopped them to the right size, and cut notches with his knife so he could connect them with two short crossbars. He bound the wood pieces together with strong vines in an H shape. He covered the top bar with vines and bark to make it more comfortable.

"Can I try it?" asked Brill eagerly.

"It's only half-finished. You need two, you know."

When he finished the second, he brought the crutches to Brill and helped him up. Brill found he could walk without putting any weight on his sore foot, but he had to be careful where he set the tips of his crutches. Ash covered the ground, and he couldn't tell how deep it was in any particular place. He fell a few times before he got used to them.

After a scanty meal, Brill hobbled over to Stargull and sat. Chela had placed an herb poultice* on the bird's burned wing, but he looked up at Brill with mournful green eyes as if to say, "What good is a bird who can't fly?"

"You'll be better soon," whispered Brill.

In the late afternoon the searchers returned with no news about Ulat or the queen.

This time even crusty Ashmi seemed sad. "Poor Father! He was a good man. I'm sorry I got impatient with him when he couldn't remember things."

They were all silent a while. "I'm hungry," said Zack. "Let's eat."

Ashmi said sharply, "Tomorrow you'll be expected to help gather food."

Zack shrugged. "Sure, I'll help."

After their meal Chela replaced the herb poultices on Brill's foot and on Stargull's wing.

Brill whispered to Stargull, "You *have* to fly so you can take a message to Segra to tell her Julnie and I are all right."

But Stargull closed his eyes as if to say, "Don't depend on me."

The next day Wokper made crutches for Julnie.

She had been very quiet. When Brill took the crutches to her, she shook her head and cringed back against the log by her shelter. "I'm afraid I'll fall."

"Crutches are tricky to get used to, but using them is a lot better than expecting to be waited on."

He cleared the sticks and rocks from a level area so Julnie would have a safe place to practice. By the end of the day she could go short distances.

When the searchers returned, Julnie called, "Look, Chela, I can walk with my new crutches."

Chela ran over to her. "That's great."

"Any news of Mother? Or Ulat?"

Chela shook her head. "The men have given up. We've looked every place on this side of the big river, but found no trace of anyone." Tears rolled from her dark eyes.

At that moment the ground shook, and an ominous gray cloud arose from Puffire.

"Oh, no! Another eruption!" screamed Julnie.

"Maybe it's only a little one," said Brill.

The cloud grew and soon ash fell on them like rain.

"That settles it," declared Ashmi. "Tomorrow we move farther south. Lilies and lizards, I'm tired of ashy food and water."

"Papa, we can't move now. Brill and Julnie can't get along by themselves yet," said Chela.

Gurat added, "If Ulat survived, he'll expect to find us here."

"Not much chance of Ulat returning," said Ashmi. He looked at Brill and Julnie. "We made crutches for the big people. They can gather their own food."

Wokper put his hand on his shoulder. "Ashmi, your own father may be out there somewhere, trying to find his way back here. We have to give him more time."

"I'm the chief here, and I give the orders. We'll leave in a few days."

Julnie whispered, "How will we survive alone? We don't know where to find edible plants."

"We can learn," Brill answered. "Chela will show us."

Ashmi didn't mention moving for the next few days,

but he grumbled a lot. "Mice and mites, I hate this ash. Why did my parents name me Ashmi? I hate my name!"

One day ash and rain fell together to make a mud shower. Brill was glad to crawl into his tiny shelter. Falling mud was worse than falling ash.

Brill began to follow Chela as she gathered food. He was learning the names of plants growing near the camp. Chela showed him a little white mushroom. "Good eating," she said. But then she pointed to another white mushroom. "This is poisonous," she warned.

"But they look the same," cried Brill.

Chela tried to point out the small differences, but Brill decided to avoid mushrooms. A mistake could be fatal.

New Arrival 10

Almost two months passed. Ashmi continued to talk about moving, but the others convinced him to wait with the slim hope that Ulat might still be alive. Ash showers fell less frequently, and there were no more eruptions like the big one.

Brill was impatient to return to Exitorn. There they would get help to look for Queen Herla. His foot had healed, and Wokper had made him a boot from rabbit skin. The Zinders did not kill animals, but they sometimes used the hide of a dead animal.

Brill was haunted by the remarks he had overheard in the palace about Segra marrying Oplack. He thought of writing a note to Segra and asking Stargull to carry it to her. But he wasn't sure Stargull could make such a long flight. Stargull spent most of his time on trees near the camp, and Brill feared that he would never be able to fly as well as he once did.

Julnie had discarded her crutches, but she still limped and refused to walk any great distance.

Brill spoke impatiently one morning as he washed in the stream. "I need to get back to Exitorn."

Julnie answered, "I want to look for Mother, too, but I can't walk over the mountains yet."

"I don't think you're eating enough. That's why you don't have any strength."

"I hate Zinder food. Am I turning green from eating all those raw plants?"

"You're not green, but you're a lot thinner."

"You too. Sometimes I dream I'm about to eat a piece of bread and honey, but I always wake up before I can take the first bite."

"We'll never get better food until we get away from here. We have to leave!"

She looked at the mountains standing between her and Brislan. "I wish we had a horse."

"Poor Comet. There's not much chance I'll ever see her again." Brill's face clouded as he again remembered his faithful horse. "We'll just have to use our feet. We'll walk slowly. Keep thinking of the bread and honey at the end."

Suddenly Chela shouted, "Grandfather! Is it really you?"

"Ulat!" Brill exclaimed. He scrambled up and joined the others who surrounded the old man. His bark clothes were tattered, and his thin hair hung in ashy strands from the edges of his bald spot.

"Papa, where have you been?" demanded Ashmi.

"We've been so worried," added Tala.

Wokper nodded toward a log. "Sit down and rest."

Ulat sat down. "Oh, I'm glad to be home. Water, please. My throat is scratchy . . . ash . . . I've been swallowing ash."

Chela ran to the stream and returned with a wooden cup full of water.

Ulat gulped it down while everyone sat on the ground to hear his story.

"Would you like something to eat?" asked Tala.

"No, thank you. I've been chewing zimba roots."

Neba leaned closer. "Do you have zimba roots?"

Ulat pulled an ashy root from his pocket. "Here, Neba. You'd better wash it first."

"Thank you!" She ran to the stream.

Ashmi scowled at his father. "Why didn't you come home sooner? We've been worrying and searching for you."

"You'll understand when you hear my story. And I'd better tell it before I forget the details. Then I'll take a long nap." A surprised expression crossed his wrinkled face. "Brill, is that you?" He had not noticed him before.

"Yes, and this is Princess Julnie."

"Princess Julnie?" Ulat repeated with a frown.

"Yes, that's my name."

"Falling firs! I should have listened to those men more carefully. They talked about a Princess Julnie."

"What men? What do you mean?" Brill asked.

"I better start at the beginning. Flashing fleas, I've had a fearful adventure. I started out one day to look for zimba roots. A forest on the other side of the river has a big patch of zimba plants. Sometimes I sneak across the bridge when it's dark and no big people are around."

"Papa! Everyone is to stay away from the big people's land," exclaimed Ashmi.

"I know, but I was always careful not to let anyone see me. I never expected that volcano to erupt like that. I crawled in a hole under a big rock when it started. That protected me from the hot wind and the falling trees. I didn't dare come out until the next day. I struggled back to the river through ash almost up to my shoulders. But the bridge was gone, and the river was a lot wider and full of mud and fallen trees. There was no way to cross it."

"Were you scared?" asked little Neba.

"Never been so scared in my life," he answered. "There I was—marooned in big people country, all alone! I sneaked among the fallen trees as I searched for a forest that was still green, where I could find food and water. It was as if I had been dropped into a terrible dead world where no food grew and the only thing to drink was gray mud. I thought I was going to die."

"What about the men you talked about?" asked Brill.

"The men? Oh yes, I'm getting to that. I finally came to a small village and found some grain that wasn't buried in ash. I picked a stalk, shook the ash off, and ate some, but then the farmer saw me and threw rocks at me."

Ashmi frowned. "Big people are mean."

"Not all of them," reminded Brill.

"I ran away from the farmer. Finally, I found a maple tree and climbed it. I don't like to get too high up, but I didn't want any rock throwers to see me. At night I crept to a farmer's well and let down a small bucket for a drink and picked a few stalks of grain.

"I was always afraid someone would catch me, so one night I left, determined to find a green forest. A day later, I found a patch of woods with zimba roots and other good food. I climbed a cedar and slept on a thick branch."

"Did you miss us?" asked Neba.

"Oh, yes. It was terrible being all alone. I didn't know if I could ever cross that river again."

"What about the men?" repeated Brill.

"I'm just getting to that part. One night some men set up camp right under my tree. They built a fire, and I was afraid the smoke was going to make me sneeze so they'd look up and see me. But I managed to keep from sneezing. They talked loudly. At first I didn't pay much attention to what they were saying. Big people's affairs don't concern me. But I pricked up my ears when they mentioned Brill. Could it be the Brill I knew?"

"What did they say?" cried Julnie impatiently.

"I'm trying to remember the details." Ulat scratched his bald head. "Somebody named Vashton got killed in the eruption, but his son—can't remember his name—"

"Kadbar," supplied Julnie.

"Yah, that's it. How do you know?"

"He's my cousin."

"Anyway, these fellows I heard wanted to have Prince Kadbar rule them. But some other fellows wanted another king. I can't remember his name either."

"Was it Trant?" asked Julnie.

"Might have been. They talked about a Princess Julnie they wanted to find, and how she went off with a fellow named Brill." He turned to Brill. "I guess they *were* talking about you."

"Did they say anything about Queen Herla?" cried Julnie. "Is she alive?"

"Herla? Frosty frogs, they mentioned so many names. I think they did talk about Herla. But by then I was feeling sleepy and wishing they'd stop talking so I could sleep."

"Try to remember more, Ulat," begged Julnie.

"I do remember one thing more. The people who don't like Kadbar control some big town. I can't remember the name."

"Was it Roxtan?" asked Julnie.

"No—no, I don't think that was it."

"How about Mulang?"

"That sounds like it. These fellows were talking about getting all the soldiers who worked for Vashton to march against Mulang."

Julnie cried, "O Brill, we have to warn them of the plot against them. Mother might even be there."

Ulat shook his head. "These men were trying to find *you*, Julnie. Don't go across that river!"

"How'd you cross the river?" asked Ashmi.

"They've put up a temporary bridge. I sneaked over one dark night. Sure was glad to get out of Brislan . . . Be quiet now so I can take a nap." Ulat curled up beside the log where he had been sitting.

The others dropped their voices. "We must have a special dinner tonight to honor Ulat," said Tala.

"I intend to point out that he got into trouble because he disobeyed orders," mumbled Ashmi.

Chela looked down at Ulat. "It's so wonderful to have Grandfather back."

Tala took Chela's hand. "Come, we need to gather

extra food for tonight."

Julnie walked to the stream and back. "I think I'm ready for a long hike," she said to Brill.

"How far is Mulang from here?"

"Quite a ways. We have to cross most of Brislan. Mulang is near the western border."

Brill thought a moment. "It's a good thing Ulat warned us about men looking for us. Otherwise we would have asked questions about your mother, and your enemies would have found us easily."

"I don't think they'll recognize me now. I look more like a poor beggar than a princess."

"I guess we will blend in with the peasants."

"I hope Ulat's memory is right, and the people who support Trant are in Mulang. They should know what happened to Mother."

"I wonder if the men who grabbed your mother were on your side. Do you think that's possible?"

"Anything's possible. Our friends would need someone to fight for. With Trant in Exitorn they may be rallying around Mother."

"By now Trant may have returned to Brislan. He was very concerned about you and your mother," said Brill. "Shall we start tomorrow morning?"

Julnie nodded. "I'm eager to find my family. But I'm scared of Kadbar."

"We'll keep out of his way." But Brill felt a shiver of fear run up his backbone.

That evening everyone sat in a circle and ate a dinner with an ample supply of mushrooms, nuts, and berries in addition to their regular leaves and roots.

Ashmi patted his full stomach and arose. "Now that we're all together again, I think we should move away from Puffire."

They argued whether to go north to the forests of Magra or south to Asperita.

Zack said, "If we go south, we might find my tribe. They travel between the forests near Brislan and Asperita."

"I'd like to see my friends from the old days," said Wokper. "I was sorry when we split into two groups."

"Orkel's tribe was a stubborn bunch," muttered Ashmi. "They wouldn't even learn to read or write."

"We didn't want to be like big people," retorted Zack.

Chela frowned. "But it helps to have instructions for preparing medicines written down."

Tala added, "We are all Zinders. Even if we differ on some things, we could still live close to one another." After much discussion the group voted to head south.

Brill spoke up. "Thank you all for taking care of Julnie and me when we couldn't walk. Without you, we would have died. We'll always remember your kindness."

Later Ulat called Brill aside. "Don't let those bad fellows find Julnie," he warned.

"I'll try to keep her safe," he promised.

"Her life won't be worth much if she falls into their hands. They're determined to make this Kadbar king. They're trying to wipe out the people in Julnie's family."

Brill gulped. He wondered if he and Julnie should go with the Zinders to the Asperitan forests and try to get back to Exitorn that way. But that would be a much longer journey, and the Asperitans were not friendly to strangers. The best plan was to sneak across Brislan to the city of Mulang where perhaps they'd find friends.

"Thanks for the warning," he said. "We'll be very careful."

The next day the Zinders left. Brill and Julnie waved to them as they crossed the stream and disappeared into the trees.

Stargull flew to the top of a hemlock tree.

Brill looked at Julnie. "Time for us to go too."

"I'm scared, Brill. I don't want to risk being locked up again."

"Do you want to stay here and eat leaves and roots?"

"That might be better than meeting Kadbar's men." She sighed. "But I have to find Mother."

"And after you get back to your people, I'm returning to Exitorn." Brill thought longingly of seeing Segra again. But danger had to be faced before he could go home.

* * * * *

Segra slipped away from the busy wedding preparations to climb her favorite castle tower. *I feel as if I'm in a play, playing the role of a happy bride.* She reached the top and looked toward Brislan. *I wonder where Brill is buried.*

Wiping tears from her eyes, she looked down at her own country. *But I will be a good queen when that day comes,* she promised.

She descended the stone stairs and met her mother in the hall.

"There you are," Queen Nalane said. "Hara was looking for you to discuss plans for the wedding reception."

"Oh—yes," said Segra slowly. "I'll go to Aunt Hara now, and ask her to include cook's good spice cake at the reception. I think Oplack will like that."

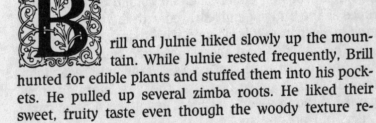

Brill and Julnie hiked slowly up the mountain. While Julnie rested frequently, Brill hunted for edible plants and stuffed them into his pockets. He pulled up several zimba roots. He liked their sweet, fruity taste even though the woody texture required a lot of chewing.

Finally they reached the top of the pass.

"Brislan still looks gray," complained Julnie as she looked at the land beyond the river.

"It'll take a while to get rid of the ash."

"I wish I knew if Mother is alive." She wiped away a tear. "I guess I'll go to Exitorn if we don't find her."

"We still have to cross Brislan to get to the road to Exitorn," pointed out Brill.

"I hope we don't run into Kadbar or his men. Kadbar's mean. Once he pushed my cat out of a tower window. If she hadn't managed to get her claws into a wooden beam, she would have been smashed on the stone courtyard. Trant rescued her for me."

That night they slept near the base of the mountain. Brill tried to clear some of the ash away between two large rocks.

"That makes it fly around more," grumbled Julnie.

"I see that." Brill sat down. "Does your leg hurt?"

"A little. Mostly I'm just tired."

"Well, you can sleep over here. It has fewer pebbles."

The next day Julnie was in a more cheerful mood. They walked to the river and crossed the temporary bridge made from ropes and wooden slats and anchored to upright logs on either side. They hung onto the side ropes as the bridge gently swayed with their weight. The muddy river was still clogged with logs.

They hurried past the ash-covered ruins of Yolben and onto a dirt road that crossed farmland. That night they slept in a grove of trees. The next morning they passed through several villages. People eyed them curiously, but no one spoke.

Brill noticed that Julnie kept glancing behind them that day. "Relax," he said. "No one's paying any attention to us."

"A man is following us!"

"He's probably going the same way we are."

"No, he adjusts his pace to match ours so he stays the same distance behind."

"Oh." Brill took a deep breath. "We'd better lose him."

"How?"

"We're coming to a town. Let's find a hiding place." Brill stopped at the marketplace, and they looked at the food for sale.

Brill's mouth watered at the sight of meat pies and sweet cakes. He glanced back to see that their pursuer had stopped to buy bread.

"Quick, follow me," he whispered to Julnie. Brill ducked under a wagon loaded with live chickens. They crouched in the dirt under the smelly cart, not even daring to look out.

"What if the wagon starts to move?" asked Julnie in low tones.

"We'll be gone by then."

They heard a man shout. "Help me look for two strangers that came to town. They may be rebels! A boy and a girl."

This warning was followed by running feet and shouts. "We'll find them," hollered a deep voice.

Julnie clutched Brill's hand. "They're looking for us."

Brill's heart pounded as he tried to think of a plan of escape. If they stayed, they'd be found, but if they tried to move, they'd be seen. How could he protect Julnie?

A muffled cry escaped from Julnie's throat as a whiskered face peered at them under the wagon. "Here they are!" he yelled. Rough hands pulled Brill and Julnie into the open.

"We found the rebels!" called the man who clutched Brill.

"We aren't rebels," explained Brill. "We're travelers on our way to Exitorn."

A woman stepped close to Julnie. "She isn't an ordinary traveler. Her gown may be worn, but look at the lace." She stared at Julnie's locket. "And peasants don't wear gold jewelry. I think this is the lost princess!"

"Tie 'em up, and we'll take 'em to Kadbar. We'll be well rewarded," said a plump fellow.

"It'll soon be dark, and I'm not taking my horse across the rocky hills at night," said a tall fellow. "We'll leave at dawn."

"We can put them in our jail overnight," suggested another man.

"She's a rebel, and they all get treated alike," answered Julnie's captor. "Get me some rope."

People crowded around to get a better look at the captives.

Someone brought a coil of rope, and the men tied Brill and Julnie's wrists and ankles. They were carried to the one-room jail and dumped without ceremony on the dirt floor. Two guards were assigned to watch the door.

Brill looked around the stone room.

"What shall we do?" whispered Julnie.

"Maybe we can talk your cousin into letting us go to Exitorn."

"He'll never agree. As long as I'm alive, I'm a threat to his throne."

Brill hobbled to the small barred window. A white bird perched on the house roof across the street. Stargull! He had flown across the mountains. Brill could see the two guards sitting with their backs against the door.

"You watch while I take a nap," one was saying.

The other yawned. "Not much to watch. I helped build the jail, and nobody's going to escape from it."

Brill looked up at Stargull. If only he could take a message to Julnie's supporters in Mulang.

He hobbled over to Julnie. "Stargull's outside. Do you have anything that your mother would recognize—if she's in Mulang?"

"Why?"

"To let her know you're alive."

"My gold locket."

"If I give that to Stargull, he can take it to Mulang."

"But how will Mother know where I am?"

"Stargull will lead her men here."

Julnie frowned. "Are you sure Stargull will understand all this?"

"I'm sure. Besides, it's our only chance." Brill tried unsuccessfully to unfasten Julnie's locket with his bound hands.

Julnie yanked it off, breaking the delicate gold chain. "It can be repaired." They hobbled to the window.

Brill glanced at the guards. They looked as if they were both napping. He waved his bound hands to Stargull, who flew to the sill. Brill held out the locket. "Take this to Mulang." He turned to Julnie. "How will he find Mulang?"

"It's the largest town on the western border," she whispered. "It has a stone church with a tall bell tower. If Mother is there, she'll be at the governor's large house on the hill."

Taking the locket in his talons, Stargull flew away.

Julnie sighed, "I hope whoever finds the locket sees my name engraved on the back."

Brill sat beside Julnie. "I know it seems like a long

shot, but it might work." He began trying to pick apart the ropes that held his ankles, but stopped. He could never finish before tomorrow, when they were to be taken to Kadbar.

Could help come in time? Did the rebels have enough men to fight Kadbar's men? Questions swirled in Brill's mind.

It grew dark, but Brill still didn't sleep. He prayed, *Lord, You've helped me many times, and I'm thankful. Please help Julnie and her country. Save it from the rule of the selfish Kadbar.*

He finally fell asleep, but awoke to hear men whispering. He had no idea what time it was.

Soon the door flew open and men entered the darkness. "Princess Julnie? Brill? We've come to rescue you. Where are you?" came a whisper.

"Over here." Brill's heart beat with excitement.

"Can't use lights. We knocked out the guards and took their keys. We're locking them inside so they can't give an alarm when they come to."

Strong men lifted Brill and Julnie and carried them out of the jail to their horses. In the faint starlight men cut their ropes.

"Is my mother all right?" cried Julnie.

"She's fine. Don't talk until we get away from here," cautioned a tall man.

Men lifted them onto horses behind riders already mounted. The six horsemen stole quietly out of the town. Then as soon as they passed all the town's houses, their horses broke into a gallop.

"Hang on tight," called a talkative man who shared a horse with Brill. "My name's Wilbun. I was on guard duty when the bird swooped down and left the locket at my feet. When I saw the name *Julnie* on the back, I took it to the queen. She got excited when she heard a white bird had brought it. She said it must be the bird you had told her about, and that he could lead us to you."

"His name's Stargull, and he's helped me before," answered Brill.

"He's smart all right. He led us right to where you were." Wilbun added in a serious tone, "We need to get as far as possible before morning when they'll come after us."

Shivers ran down Brill's spine. He glanced back, but he couldn't see anything beyond the rescue party. Dawn came and still the road remained empty. Hope beat in Brill's heart, and he began to feel even more confident as the sun mounted in the sky.

Wilbun must have been confident too, for he eased the pace a little. "We need to spare our tired horses," he explained.

"Pursuers!" suddenly yelled one of the men behind Brill.

Brill twisted to look. A cloud of ash billowed in the road far behind.

They again pounded down the road at a fast gallop. Julnie's horse spurted ahead as the rider called, "We can't let them capture the princess."

Brill looked back to see the ominous cloud coming closer. Kadbar's men were gaining on them!

Brill gulped. "I could help fight if I had a sword."

"I only have one sword, but I'll try to protect us with that. There's Mulang's bell tower up ahead, but we can't outrun Kadbar's men. Their horses are fresher than ours."

Brill squinted against the sun and saw another

band of riders galloping from the direction they were heading. He took a deep breath and tried to control the fear that sent painful pricks from nerve to nerve.

"We're surrounded!" he exclaimed.

He felt as if his neck were on a spring as he tried to watch the horsemen approaching from both directions.

Then the riders from the city passed them with shouts of, "Keep going! We'll handle the enemy."

"They're ours," yelled Wilbun. "The lookout from the bell tower saw we were in trouble."

Brill looked back to see the battle, but Kadbar's men turned and galloped away to escape from the large rebel force. A great relief washed over him. *Thank You, Lord,* he whispered.

They rode into the fair-sized town, where a few people were already coming out to greet them. Brill felt like part of a parade as they followed the street up a hill to a large stone house.

Queen Herla and Prince Trant rushed outside to greet them. As Julnie dismounted, the queen hugged her. "My dearest one, I'm so glad to see you!" Tears of joy ran down the queen's cheeks. "I sent men to search for you, but they couldn't find you. We all thought you had been swept away by the mudflow." She kissed Julnie, and then stood back to look at her. "You're so thin! Where have you been all this time?"

"I'll tell you later, Mother. Oh, it's *so* good to be with you again." She looked down at her ragged clothes. "Please, could Brill and I change and wash up and have some bread and honey? If it hadn't been for Brill, I wouldn't be here. He pulled me out of the river and carried me when I couldn't walk."

Queen Herla shook Brill's hand. "Thank you for all

you've done."

Trant patted him on the back. "Thanks, Brill."

Brill nodded, then looked around for Stargull. He didn't see him. Brill hoped he had found a tree to rest in after the longest flights he had made since the big eruption.

Later, as they sat down to a lunch of sliced chicken, fruit, and bread and honey, Julnie and Brill related their adventures to the queen and Trant.

"Now tell me what happened to you," said Julnie to her mother.

"As Ulfa and I walked toward the river, a band of men grabbed me, pulled me onto a horse, and galloped away. My heart almost stopped beating until I recognized the voice of one of your father's servants. He was wearing a mask to keep out the ash."

"Who was it?" asked Julnie.

"It was Wilbun. When we got away from the city, he apologized for scaring me. He and his men want to restore someone from our family to the throne. They brought me to Mulang. By then we heard Vashton was dead and Kadbar had proclaimed himself king. At first they didn't tell anyone I was here for fear Kadbar would try to kill me."

Trant added, "The good men of Brislan are working to overthrow Kadbar and his evil companions. We control the southwest area of Brislan, and more villages are gradually joining our side. But it will take a war to decide who rules Brislan."

Julnie said, "One of our friends overheard plans for Kadbar's men to march against Mulang."

"Mulang is well defended," answered Trant, "and we're planning to invade Roxtan, which our enemies are using for their capital."

Julnie looked at her brother. "Will you rule if our side wins?"

Trant nodded. "They've asked me to be king. These men loved our father, and they feel I can carry on his good work."

Julnie took another piece of bread and spread it with butter and honey. "This is what I missed most when I lived with the Zinders. I don't think I'll ever eat another green thing."

Brill turned to Queen Herla. "I would like to return to Exitorn. King Silgar will want to know the outcome of my mission."

"I'll miss you," cried Julnie.

Brill looked at the princess. What was she thinking?

The queen said, "Julnie, I think you should go with Brill. Things are very uncertain here with both sides preparing for war. It would make me feel better if I knew you were safe. If anything happens to Trant or me, you'll be the one to carry on Choner's line. An assassin* has already tried to kill Trant. Luckily his arrow missed its mark, and our men captured him."

Julnie said brightly, "I would like to meet my cousin Segra."

"After you've rested a few days, we'll send an armed escort to take you and Brill over the mountains."

Brill smiled. He had assumed he'd be walking that long way. On horseback the trip would go much faster, and he'd see Segra sooner. Trant had told him about the Exitornian soldiers who were sent to search for him and Julnie. They must have told King Silgar that Julnie and he had been killed in the eruption. Segra would be surprised to see him.

A Shock 12

Segra stood on a stool as the dressmaker pinned up the hem of her ivory wedding dress. Tiny flowers of gold thread covered the flowing sleeves.

"Segra, you'll be the most beautiful bride this kingdom has ever seen," exclaimed her mother, Nalane.

"Everything is ready for the welcoming banquet for Prince Oplack and his family," added Aunt Hara.

Segra forced a smile. In two weeks she'd be married to Oplack. She prayed, *Lord, I'm doing what is best for my country. Why can't I feel happy?*

"The hem is pinned," said the dressmaker. She

carefully pulled the dress over Segra's head.

"Let's climb the west tower and see if we can spot the royal ship of Leoniff," suggested Rima.

"All right," Segra agreed as she slipped into a lavender gown. *I wish I could share everyone's joy,* she thought as she followed Rima up the circular staircase of the stone tower.

Segra scanned the skies, hoping to see Stargull, but she only saw a few black crows.

Rima pointed. "I see a sailing ship. I think that's it!" She looked at Segra and frowned. "You're not playing your role of happy bride very well."

"Does it show?"

"Of course it shows. That silly smile you paste on occasionally wouldn't fool anyone. Segra, why did you agree to marry Oplack if you hate him?"

"I don't hate him! I like him very much—only I still love Brill."

"But Brill's dead."

"I know. And it's best for my country to marry Oplack. I can't let anyone know how I really feel." Segra blinked back tears. Why were emotions so unruly? She wanted to forget her love for Brill and be happy. Why was it so difficult?

Rima said, "More wedding guests are coming, but I don't recognize the uniforms of the escorting soldiers."

Segra yawned and looked down at the bridge that crossed the moat. All at once her knees felt weak, and she clung to the stone battlements. "That looks like Brill."

"That man in the middle? His hair is brown, but you can't see his face from here. He's not riding Comet."

Segra's heart pounded in her temples. "But I know

it's Brill."

"He was killed in the eruption," repeated Rima.

Segra spun around and hurried down the stairs. By the time she and Rima arrived in the throne room, a page was announcing the names of the new arrivals.

"Princess Julnie of Brislan and Duke Brill of Exitorn," he called.

The king greeted the princess and Brill warmly.

Segra stood with paralyzed legs. *Brill! Alive!* Oh, it was wonderful—but she was engaged to be married to the wrong man!

Brill ran to her and grasped both her hands. "It's marvelous to see you," he exclaimed.

"I'm very glad you're alive," she whispered, fighting tears of both happiness and despair.

Brill said, "And this is your cousin Julnie. She's been looking forward to meeting you."

Segra looked at the beautiful princess. Perhaps Brill . . . But of course not. Segra smiled and stepped forward to hug her cousin. "I hoped we could meet someday."

"Sit down and tell us about your adventures," invited the king.

Segra sank into a chair and tried to concentrate on Brill's tale. But part of her mind was racing. She couldn't marry Oplack—not now. She stared at Brill and dreamed for a few minutes of walking down the cathedral aisle to meet him as her groom. But the wedding was only two weeks away. It was too late to stop it!

* * * * *

When Brill and Julnie finished their story, King

Silgar said, "Brill, your old room is just as you left it. Rima, please tell the housekeeper to prepare the room next to Segra's for Julnie."

Rima curtsied and left.

The king turned to Brill and Julnie. "Tonight we're having a banquet to welcome Prince Oplack and the king and queen of Leoniff. It's the beginning of the wedding festivities leading to Oplack and Segra's wedding two weeks from now."

Brill suddenly felt as if a wave of icy seawater had doused his happiness. He stood and bowed before the king. "With your permission, Your Majesty, I'm going to my room." He forced himself to sound cheerful.

As he left, he heard Julnie exclaim, "I'm so glad we arrived in time for your wedding. I love weddings."

When he reached his room, he paced the floor. Segra didn't love him, or she wouldn't have agreed to marry Oplack. How could he watch the wedding? Perhaps he'd go back to Brislan. Or maybe he'd live with the Zinders—anyplace but here!

He answered the knock on his door.

A servant said, "Your bath is ready."

"I didn't order a bath." he snapped.

"It's customary after a long journey, sir." Brill grabbed his robe and stalked toward the bathing room.

When he returned, he flipped through the tunics in his wardrobe, passing by the bright colors and selecting a plain gray one. He hesitated. Maybe he'd say he was too tired to attend the banquet. . . .

But on a sudden impulse, he went to Segra's room to offer his congratulations. He realized he had been too stunned to say anything to her when he first heard the news.

Segra opened the door, "Hello, Brill." She wore a deep blue gown that matched her eyes.

She was beautiful, and that chased all Brill's rehearsed words from his mind. He blurted out, "You can't marry Oplack! You love me."

Segra stiffened. "You forget yourself. I am a princess and I must marry a prince."

"Segra, at least be honest with me."

She stepped back, then covered her face with her hands and began to sob.

Brill put his arms around her. "I'm sorry. I didn't mean to make you cry." He pulled her close. "I love you."

Through her sobs she said, "I thought you were dead. Oh Brill, I love you, not Oplack, but it's too late. All the plans are set."

"There must be some way to stop the wedding!" But even as Brill spoke, he realized that if Segra rejected Oplack, it might trigger an international crisis.

Gently, Brill released Segra, his hands lingering on her shoulders. "I'll always love you, Segra."

He left to return to his room. Part of his heart sang, "Segra loves me," but the other part moaned, "It's too late."

At the banquet Brill sat by Julnie. She looked beautiful in a green satin gown decorated with pearls. Guests lifted their glasses in a toast to her and then in a toast to the future bride and groom.

After dinner a jester* performed. Laughter filled the room. Only Brill and Segra were miserable.

The next day Brill visited Grossder at the cathedral. They shared all that had happened to them since they had been separated by King Vashton, but Brill didn't talk about the pain in his heart.

During the next few days parties honored the bridal couple. Delegations arrived from Magra and from some of the tribes of Asperita. Old quarrels were forgotten as the great celebration drew closer.

A troop of soldiers came from Brislan to report that Kadbar had been killed in the first battle of the civil war.* The opposition had surrendered, and Trant had been proclaimed king.

"That's wonderful news," said Julnie.

"You can return to Brislan," said Brill.

"I don't want to go back just yet."

"Maybe after the wedding."

Julnie scowled. "Maybe."

"Don't you want to go home?" asked Brill.

She sighed and didn't answer. Brill shrugged. What was wrong with Julnie?

At the end of the week, Brill decided to visit his parents in Grebing near the mountains. He hadn't seen them since last spring when they visited the palace. He just couldn't watch Segra marry someone else. She would understand why he was leaving.

As Brill began to pack, Segra knocked on his door. "I need to talk to you," she began, stepping inside. She looked at his pile of clothes. "What are you doing?"

"I'm leaving in the morning to visit my parents."

"Brill, wait. I may have found a way out. Have you noticed anything different about Oplack?"

Brill thought a moment. "No—what?"

"Haven't you seen how he looks at Julnie and how much time he spends with her?"

"What are you getting at?"

"I think Oplack has fallen for Julnie. Brill, please

talk to Oplack. Find out how he feels."

"Do you think he'd call off the wedding?"

"That's what I'm praying." She smiled. "Tell him I won't be brokenhearted."

"I'll find Oplack right away." Brill felt tingles of excitement race through his body. But perhaps Segra was only imagining things—because she wanted an escape from her wedding.

Brill found Oplack and Julnie eating peaches in the orchard. Julnie crooned, "Oplack picked me the sweetest peach in the whole orchard."

As Brill picked a peach, he noticed how Julnie beamed at Oplack. Remembering her reluctance to go home, it wasn't hard to believe she loved Oplack, but he couldn't decide from watching Oplack's grim face how *he* felt. Perhaps he was annoyed that Brill had intruded on his time alone with Julnie.

"Good peaches," said Brill as he bit into one.

"Wonderful," agreed Julnie, wiping her sticky hands on a leaf. She stood. "Well, I have to change my clothes for dinner. I'll see you later."

As she walked toward the castle, Brill turned to Oplack. "Julnie's very pretty."

"Beautiful," agreed Oplack.

"How do you feel about her?"

"What kind of question is that? I'm getting married in a week."

Brill shrugged and tried to sound casual. "I've noticed you spend quite a bit of time with her."

Oplack countered with his own question. "Are you in love with Julnie?"

"Me? No, of course not."

Oplack spoke slowly. "I admit I wish I had met

Julnie sooner. Segra seems aloof—as if she doesn't even like me. But it's too late to change plans now."

"Maybe not," said Brill.

"Have you talked to Segra?" asked Oplack.

"She noticed that you seemed interested in Julnie."

"Was she angry?"

"No. Segra's in love with someone else too. It's a tangle, Oplack. Can we sort it out before it's too late?"

"Is Segra in love with you?" demanded Oplack.

Brill nodded. "I'm sorry, but she agreed to marry you because she thought I was dead."

Oplack looked where Julnie had gone into the castle. "I should be insulted, but I thought that was probably true. I'm going to find Julnie and make sure how she feels. Then I'll talk to my parents. There'll be a terrible fuss, but I think we must call off the wedding."

Brill hurried to Segra's room and related his conversation with Oplack. Segra exclaimed, "O Brill, if Oplack calls off the wedding, we can be married."

He felt his pulse race as he answered, "But I'm not a prince. Will your father let you marry me?"

Segra squeezed his hand. "Father wants me to be happy. I'll remind him that *he* married a goatherd's daughter because he loved her so much. Let's go talk to him now."

As they walked down the hall, they met Prince Oplack, who smiled broadly as he declared, "Julnie does love me, and I'm going to my parents' room now."

"We're on our way to talk to Father," said Segra.

Brill followed her, but his stomach cramped into a nervous ball. His whole future depended on the next few minutes.

They found the king and queen in the throne room.

As Segra explained what had happened, Brill watched the king, looking for signs of anger; but he couldn't tell what he was thinking.

At that moment Oplack entered the room with his parents. Queen Sera stormed up to the throne.

She glared at Segra. "My son's promised bride has treated him so shamefully, he was forced to make friends with another woman. Tell your daughter she must change her ways."

King Silgar said, "Let's all sit down and talk about the situation."

"Calm down, dear," whispered King Yardo.

"I can't calm down," cried Queen Sera. "We came all this way to see our son married, and now he says there may not be a wedding! We'll look like fools. The wedding has to take place as planned."

"Mother, I love Julnie," declared Oplack.

"We have always planned for you to marry the princess of Exitorn. You must not let *love* distract you from your duties as the future king of Leoniff."

"But Julnie's a princess too," reminded King Yardo. "I've been thinking that an alliance with Brislan might be a good thing."

Queen Sera shook her finger at him. "Yardo! Don't tell me you're going to agree to this embarrassing change in plans!"

King Silgar said, "Sera, we want our children to be happy. The burdens of ruling are often heavy. It has helped me to have a wife at my side whom I love." He squeezed Nalane's hand.

"What will we tell our guests?" wailed Queen Sera.

"I'll prepare a statement explaining that by mutual agreement the wedding has been cancelled." King Silgar looked at Brill. "Am I correct in assuming you want to marry Segra?"

"Oh, yes—yes, Your Majesty," stammered Brill. Excitement raced through his nerves.

"Then the wedding can take place—with Duke Brill as the groom."

Oplack said, "After Segra and Brill's wedding, Julnie and I will travel to Brislan for her brother's coronation.* With her family's permission, we'll be married there."

Queen Sera sighed. "That will mean a long journey on horseback. Why do you have to marry someone from over the mountains?"

"You don't have to go," said King Yardo.

"Not go? Of course I'll go. Oplack is my only son. Perhaps Julnie will not be as strong willed as Segra. We may get along well. Bring her here, Oplack. We must get better acquainted."

After dinner, Brill and Segra slipped off to the tower to be alone. He took both her hands and looked into her eyes. "I came so close to losing you, and I can't imagine ever being happy without you."

"I feel as if I've lost a heavy weight. I think I'm light enough to float out over the countryside." Segra squeezed his hands.

"I must write to my parents inviting them to our wedding."

"Father will send the letter by special messenger," said Segra. "Look, Brill. Here comes Stargull!"

The large white bird landed on the battlements, and Segra exclaimed, "I'm glad you can fly across the mountains again!"

Brill patted his back. "If you hadn't helped rescue Julnie and me, we might never have reached Exitorn, and four people would have missed great happiness."

"God meant for us to be together," said Segra, "and He worked it out with His perfect timing."

Brill nodded. He took Segra in his arms, hugging her close and kissing her. "Life will always be a wonderful adventure with you."

LIFE IN EXITORN

Abbot: The head of a monastery or abbey.

Ash: Powder-like rock from a volcano. The rock turns to powder from the force of the eruption.

Assassin: A murderer who kills a well-known person, especially one involved with government.

Avalanche: A mass of earth, rocks, or snow suddenly and swiftly sliding down a mountain.

Battlements: Low walls with open spaces for shooting

built on top of buildings such as castles or forts.

Betrothed: Engaged to be married.

Cantankerous: Bad-tempered, quarrelsome.

Cathedral: A large important church where a bishop presides.

Civil war: War between two groups of people from the same nation.

Coronation: The ceremony in which a king is crowned.

Crater: A bowl-shaped cavity, as at the top of a volcano.

Dais: A platform raised above the floor at one end of a room, as for a throne.

Debris: Rough, broken pieces of stone, wood, and other things sometimes caused by a disaster such as a hurricane or a volcanic eruption.

Dragator: Imaginary animals who live in rivers like alligators but have long necks and legs like dragons.

Eruption: A bursting forth of lava from a volcano. In some places under the surface of the earth it is so hot that rock is liquid. In an explosive eruption the force of the explosion turns lava into ash or dust.

Hose: Stockings. Long, tight pants formerly worn by men.

Jester: A person who is hired to play a fool to amuse a ruler.

Lava: Hot, melted rock flowing from a volcano. Also, rock formed by the cooling of this melted rock.

Locket: A small, hinged, ornamental case of metal for holding a picture or other item, worn suspended from a chain around the neck.

Mesa: A hill having deeply sloped sides and a level top.

Monastery: A building where monks live.

Monk: A man who separates himself from ordinary living and promises to devote his life to God.

Ogre: A hideous giant of fairy tales who eats people.

Page: A boy servant who serves in a palace.

Pallet: A thin mattress filled with straw or other material and used on the floor.

Plague: A dangerous disease that spreads rapidly and often causes death.

Portcullis: A heavy iron grating suspended by chains and lowered between grooves to bar the gateway of a castle or fortress.

Poultice: A soft, moist mass of herbs applied to a sore part of the body.

Spire: The top part of a tower or steeple that narrows to a point.

Stargull: A large white seabird with eagle-like talons. Stargull cannot talk, but he understands human speech.

Suite: A group of connected rooms used as a unit.

Sulfur: A light-yellow, nonmetallic element that burns easily, producing a stifling odor. It is common in volcanic regions.

Vespers: An evening church service.

Wily: Sly, crafty.